This book
belongs to

....

50 UTTERLY FUNNY STORIES

Compiled by **Vic Parker**

Miles Kelly

First published in 2016 by Miles Kelly Publishing Ltd
Harding's Barn, Bardfield End Green, Thaxted, Essex, CM6 3PX, UK

2 4 6 8 10 9 7 5 3 1

Publishing Director Belinda Gallagher
Creative Director Jo Cowan
Editorial Director Rosie Neave
Editor Amy Johnson
Senior Designer Rob Hale
Production Elizabeth Collins, Caroline Kelly
Reprographics Stephan Davis, Jennifer Cozens, Thom Allaway

ISBN 978-1-78209-995-6

Printed in China

British Library Cataloguing-in-Publication Data
A catalogue record for this book is available from the British Library

ACKNOWLEDGEMENTS

The publishers would like to thank the following
artists who have contributed to this book:
Advocate Art: Stevee Stone (including cover and decorative frames)
Beehive Illustration: Mike Phillips
The Bright Agency: Kathryn Durst, Michael Garton
Milan Illustrations Agency: Tina Perko
Plum Pudding: Mirella Mariani

The publishers would like to thank the following sources
for the use of their photographs:
Shutterstock.com (endpapers) Magnia

Made with paper from a sustainable forest
www.mileskelly.net

CONTENTS

Animal Antics

Fantastic Fools

Trickster Tales

Crazy Capers

Absurd Accidents

Animal Antics

The Hare and the Tortoise

An Aesop's fable

A hare was once boasting to the other animals about how speedy he was.

"No one is faster than me," he said with a smirk. "I challenge anyone to prove me wrong – who is bold enough to race me?"

Of course, no one dared put themselves forward… until a tortoise slowly lifted his head and spoke. "I accept your challenge," the old, wrinkled one announced softly.

The hare burst out laughing. "Oh, that

is funny, please tell me you are joking."

But the tortoise was deadly serious. "Save your boasting until you've beaten me," he replied.

The other animals, astonished, rushed to set a course. It took the tortoise several minutes to amble to the start line. Some of the animals muttered to each other and shook their heads.

"Ready, set, go!" bellowed the ox – and finally the race began.

The hare darted out of sight at once.

As soon as he had rounded the bend, he thought he'd have a laugh at the tortoise's expense. He lay down under a tree and pretended to nap – just to show that he could even stop to sleep and still beat the tortoise. But in the peaceful shade, the hare really did fall fast asleep!

Slowly, slowly, the tortoise plodded on – past the sleeping hare – until the finish line was in sight. At the sound of the animals' cheers the hare woke with a start, horrified. He bounded on, but the tortoise trudged over the finish line before him.

And the moral of the story is: slow and steady wins the race.

The Elephant's Child

Adapted from the story by Rudyard Kipling

In the High and Far-Off Times, the Elephant, O Best Beloved, had no trunk. He had only a blackish, bulgy nose, as big as a boot, which he could wriggle about from side to side.

There was one Elephant – a new Elephant, an Elephant's Child – who was full of 'satiable curtiosity, and that means he asked ever so many questions.

He filled all Africa with his 'satiable curtiosities. He asked his tall aunt, the Ostrich, why her tail-feathers grew just so, and his tall aunt the Ostrich spanked him with her sharp claws. He asked his tall uncle, the Giraffe, what made his skin spotty, and his tall uncle the Giraffe spanked him with his hard hoof. He asked his broad aunt, the Hippopotamus, why her eyes were red, and his broad aunt the Hippopotamus spanked him with her broad hoof. And he asked his hairy uncle, the Baboon, why melons tasted just so, and his hairy uncle the Baboon spanked him with his hairy paw.

The Elephant's Child

He asked questions about everything that he saw, or heard, or felt, or smelt, or touched, and all his uncles and his aunts spanked him. And still he was full of 'satiable curtiosity!

One fine morning, this 'satiable Elephant's Child asked a fine new question that he had never asked before. He asked, "What does the Crocodile have for dinner?" Then everybody said, "Hush!" and spanked him immediately and directly for a long time.

By and by, when that was finished, he came upon Kolokolo Bird sitting in the middle of a wait-a-bit thornbush, and he said, "My father has spanked me, and my mother has spanked me. All my aunts and uncles have spanked me for my 'satiable curtiosity, and still I want to know what the Crocodile has for dinner!"

Then Kolokolo Bird said, with a mournful cry, "Go to the banks of the great grey-green, greasy Limpopo River, all set about with fever-trees, and find out."

That very next morning, this 'satiable Elephant's Child said to all his dear families, "Goodbye. I am going to the great grey-green, greasy Limpopo River, all set about with fever-trees, to find out what the Crocodile has for dinner." And they all spanked him once more for luck, though he asked them most politely to stop.

Then he went away, a little warm, but not at all astonished, and at last he came to the banks of the great grey-green, greasy Limpopo River, all set about with fever-trees, precisely as Kolokolo Bird had said.

Now you must know and understand, O Best Beloved, that till that very week, and day, and hour, and minute, this 'satiable Elephant's Child had never seen a Crocodile, and did not know what one was like.

He trod on what he thought was a log of wood at the very edge of the great grey-green, greasy Limpopo River, all set about with fever-trees. But it was really the Crocodile, O Best Beloved, and the

Crocodile winked one eye – like this.

"'Scuse me," said the Elephant's Child most politely, "but do you happen to have seen a Crocodile?"

The Crocodile winked the other eye and lifted half his tail out of the mud. The Elephant's Child stepped back most politely as he did not wish to be spanked again.

"Come hither, Little One," said the Crocodile, "for I am the Crocodile." And he wept crocodile-tears to show it was quite true.

Then the Elephant's Child grew all breathless, and panted, and kneeled down on the bank and said, "You are the very person I have been looking for all these long days. Will you please tell me what you have for dinner?"

"Come hither, Little One," said the Crocodile, "and I'll whisper."

So the Elephant's Child put his head down close to the Crocodile's musky, tusky mouth, and the Crocodile caught him by his little nose, which up to that very week, day, hour, and minute, had been no bigger than a boot, though much more useful.

"I think," said the Crocodile – and he said it between his teeth, like this – "I think today I will begin with Elephant's Child!"

At this, O Best Beloved, the Elephant's Child was much annoyed, and he said, speaking through his nose like this, "Led go! You are hurtig be!" Then he sat back on his little haunches, and pulled, and pulled, and pulled, and his nose began to stretch. The Crocodile floundered into the water, making it all creamy with great sweeps of his tail, and he pulled, and pulled, and pulled. And the Elephant's Child spread all his four little legs and pulled, and pulled, and pulled, and his nose kept on stretching – and it hurt him an awful lot!

Suddenly the Elephant's Child felt his legs slipping, and he said through his nose, which was now nearly five feet long, "This is too butch for be!"

Then a Bi-Coloured-Python-Rock-Snake noticed his predicament and knotted himself tight round the hind legs of the scrambling Elephant's Child. He pulled, and the Elephant's Child pulled, and the

Crocodile pulled… but the Elephant's Child and the Bi-Coloured-Python-Rock-Snake pulled hardest. At last the Crocodile let go of the Elephant's Child's nose with a plop that you could hear all up and down the Limpopo River.

The Elephant's Child sat down most hard and sudden. First he said "Thank you" to the Bi-Coloured-Python-Rock-Snake. Next he was kind to his poor stretched nose. He wrapped it all up in cool banana leaves and dangled it in the great grey-green, greasy Limpopo River to cool.

The Elephant's Child sat there for three days waiting for his nose to shrink. But it never grew any shorter, and besides, it made him squint. For, O Best Beloved, you

will see and understand that the Crocodile
had stretched it out into a really truly trunk
same as all Elephants have today. So the
Elephant's Child went home across Africa,
frisking and whisking his trunk.

One dark evening he arrived back to all
his dear families and asked them, "How do
you do?"

"Oh bananas!" said they. "What have
you done to your nose?"

"I got a new one from the Crocodile on
the banks of the great grey-green, greasy
Limpopo River," said the Elephant's Child.
"I asked him what he had for dinner, and
he gave me this to keep."

"It looks very ugly," said his hairy uncle,
the Baboon.

"It does," said the Elephant's Child. "But it's very useful." Then that bad Elephant's Child spanked all his dear families for a long time, till they were very warm and greatly astonished.

At last, his dear families went off one by one in a hurry to the banks of the great grey-green, greasy Limpopo River, all set about with fever-trees, to borrow new noses from the Crocodile. When they came back, nobody spanked anybody any more… and ever since that day, O Best Beloved, all Elephants have trunks precisely like the trunk of the 'satiable Elephant's Child.

Brer Bear's House

Adapted from an *Uncle Remus* story
by Joel Chandler Harris

Of all the creatures in the forest, Brer
Bear had the biggest and the warmest
house. I don't know why or wherefore, but
I'm telling you the plain facts, and that's
the truth of the matter.

Brer Bear never bragged about it. And
even though his house was the biggest, it
was still on the small side for his family –
who were all rather large! Brer Bear had a

lovely plump wife named Mama Bear and a handsome plump son named Simon and a clever plump daughter named Susanna.

The Bear family always did everything together. They packed into their big dining room to eat together. They jammed into their big bathroom to wash together. They squeezed into their big living room to hang out together. And at nighttime, they squashed into the same big bedroom to sleep together.

Even though they were always treading on each other's toes and jostling each other and stumbling over each other, they loved being a big happy family together in their big warm house.

Now, one day there came a *Bang! Bang! Bang!* at Brer Bear's door. The Bear family looked at each other in surprise. *Bang! Bang! Bang!* The knocking continued – loud and mighty urgent. Whoever could it be? "Who's out there?"

growled Brer Bear, just as another *Bang! Bang! Bang!* rattled the door. "Stop bashing at my door, or else!" he roared, his voice like rumbling thunder. "Who are you and what do you want?"

"It's Brer Skunk!" came the answer in a high-pitched squeak. "Please let me in! I was hoping to come and live with you. It's so cold out here! And everyone I meet tells me how warm your big house is. I'll pay my way! I'm a hard worker and you must have lots of jobs that need doing."

Now that, Brer Bear was not expecting. "Hmmm…" he pondered. "It's true that it's mighty cold out there in the forest just now… and it's true that our house is mighty big and mighty warm… but I don't believe you, Brer Skunk. What is it that you're really wanting?"

"Honest, Brer Bear, I'm telling the truth!" came Brer Skunk's voice, his teeth chattering. "I'm such a good housekeeper that lots of forest families have asked me to go and work for them. But you're such a fine gentleman, I'd really most like to work for you."

Brer Skunk's flattery had no effect on sensible Brer Bear. "We don't need a housekeeper," he replied gruffly. "Even if we did, we haven't got room for one. We're short of space as it is. Of course, if you want to keep my house on the outside, you're welcome to do that." He chuckled at his own joke.

But Brer Skunk would not take no for an answer. "Ah," he yelled back straight away, "but I'm so good at clearing up and tidying away that even though you may think you've got no room, I can make you as much space as you want! Just let me in and I'll show you."

Now that got the Bear family thinking. How Mama Bear would love to eat at the dining table without knocking elbows with everyone else. How Susanna Bear dreamed of washing in the bathroom without getting soaked by the others' splashing. How Simon Bear imagined being able to get in and out of bed without bumping into the walls. And how Brer Bear pictured being able to stretch his legs out in the living room instead of sitting cramped in a corner.

"You're hired!" Brer Bear bellowed, and Susanna Bear sprang up to open the door.

Brer Skunk was accompanied in by a bitterly cold wind and swirling leaves. *BAM!* The door slammed shut behind him.

"Now, Brer Bear, let me show you how I can make more space," he said, with a glint in his eye. And he lifted up his bushy tail and squirted his very special scent.

"Bleuuurgh!" the Bear family cried. As the stinking smell filled their noses, everyone began to cough and choke.

Gasping for fresh air, the four bears staggered to the door, threw it open and tumbled outside. They raced off into the forest, trying to get far away from the evil

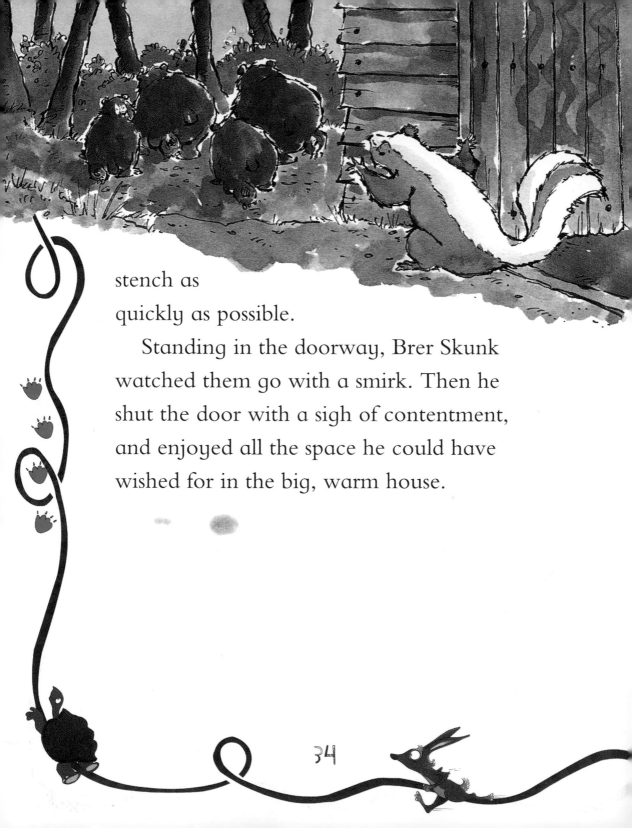

stench as
quickly as possible.

Standing in the doorway, Brer Skunk
watched them go with a smirk. Then he
shut the door with a sigh of contentment,
and enjoyed all the space he could have
wished for in the big, warm house.

Taken for a Ride

An extract from *The Talking Horse* by F Anstey

During the Victorian period, some fashionable wealthy people liked to ride horses down Rotten Row, a track in Hyde Park, London. In this story, a young man called Gustavus Pulvertoft wants to join them. He learns to ride, but with unexpected results…

I attended a fashionable riding school near Hyde Park, determined to acquire the art of horsemanship.

To say that I found learning a pleasure would be a lie. I have passed many happier hours than those I spent cantering round

four bare whitewashed walls on a snorting
horse, with my stirrups crossed upon the
saddle. The riding-master informed me
from time to time that I was getting on –
and I knew instinctively when I was
coming off. I must have made some
progress however, for as time went on he
became more and more encouraging.

I kept on trying and continually asked
my riding-master when he thought I should
be good enough to go riding in public,
down Rotten Row. After a while, he was
still not convinced, but didn't actually say
no. "It's like this, you see, sir," he
explained, "if you get hold of a quiet,
steady horse, why, you won't come to no
harm, but if you go out on a headstrong

animal, Mr Pulvertoft, why, you could get into a spot of trouble, sir."

They would have given me a horse at the school, but I knew most of the animals there, and none of them quite came up to my ideal of a quiet, steady horse. So I went to another stables nearby and asked if they had an animal that might suit me. The stable-master said that he just so happened to have one that would suit me down to the ground.

I thought the horse looked perfect. He was a chestnut of good proportions, with a sleek mane, but what reassured me was the calm look in his eye.

"You won't get a showier park 'orse than what he is, while at the same time very quiet," said his owner.

I was powerfully drawn towards the horse. He looked very intelligent and he seemed to know that he would have to be on his best behaviour if we rode in front of everyone. With hardly a second thought, I booked him for the following afternoon.

Next day, I mounted at the stables feeling a little nervous. At length, I found myself riding out into the London traffic on the back of the chestnut – whose name, by the way, was Brutus.

I shall never forget the pride and joy of having my steed under perfect control, as we turned into the park. I clucked my tongue and he immediately broke into a canter. I said "Woah" and he stopped.

When I asked him to trot, he trotted. I was
so grateful, I could have kissed him!

We had just reached Rotten Row when
– and I know you won't believe this – I
heard an unfamiliar voice addressing me
with, "I say – you there!"

The next moment, I realized it was
coming from my horse! I am not ashamed
to admit that I nearly fell off. I was too
busy trying to get my balance to
reply straight away, so the
horse spoke
again. "I say,"
he inquired, in
a rather cheeky
tone, "do you
think you can ride?"

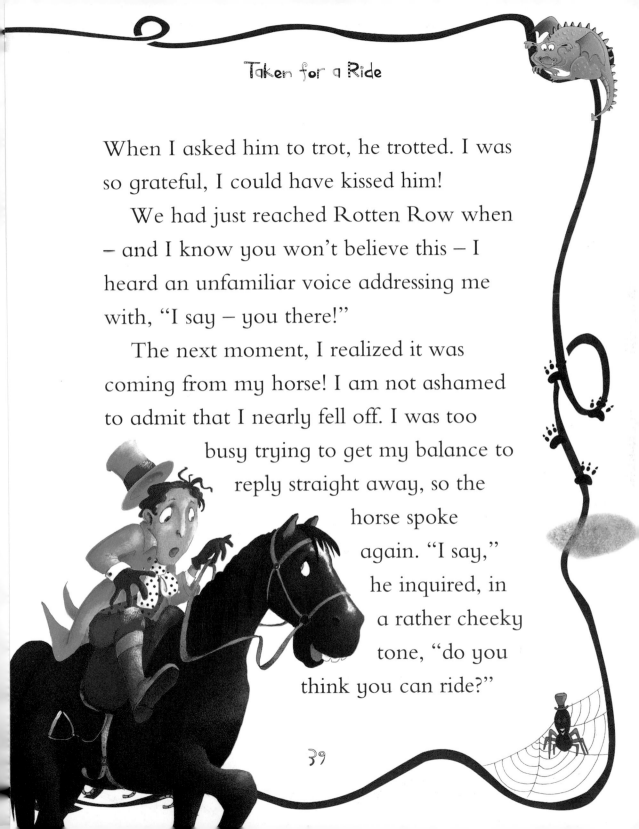

39

"If you won't stop and let me get off properly," I said with distinct firmness, "I shall roll off onto the ground."

"I will bolt away with you first," the horse replied. "You must see that you are in my power. Come, now – buy me!"

I had an idea. "If you take me back then, I will arrange it at once," I said.

Needless to say, my plan was to get safely off his back, after which nothing was going to make me buy him.

But, as we were heading back to the stables, the horse said thoughtfully, "I think it will be better if you make your offer to my owner before you dismount."

I was too vexed to speak – this clever animal had outwitted me!

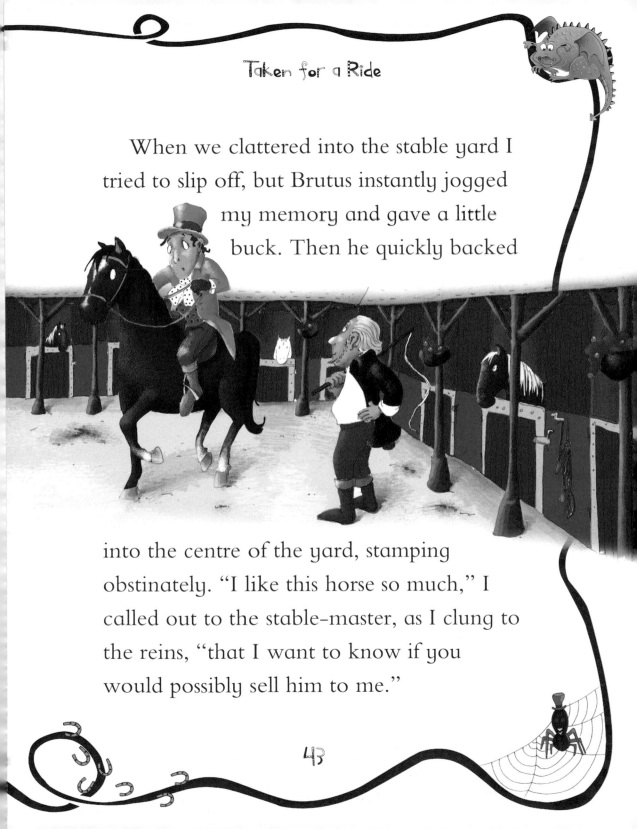

When we clattered into the stable yard I tried to slip off, but Brutus instantly jogged my memory and gave a little buck. Then he quickly backed into the centre of the yard, stamping obstinately. "I like this horse so much," I called out to the stable-master, as I clung to the reins, "that I want to know if you would possibly sell him to me."

incredibly clever and cunning that his eyes sparkled with excitement.

Anansi was going to get some common sense. Not a little bit of common sense, or even a lot of common sense – but all the common sense in the world. After all, if Anansi was the only creature with any common sense, everyone would have to come to him for advice. When they did, of course Anansi would generously share his wisdom – but charge dearly for it. How powerful Anansi would be! And how rich! He chuckled with delight at the thought.

Anansi scrutinized all the gourd trees round about until he found one growing an enormous, firm, hard-skinned fruit called a calabash. He picked the calabash, cut the

top off, and hollowed it out like a pumpkin.
Then he began searching for common
sense. He looked high and low, and
whenever he found a piece, he put it into
the calabash. He found a little common
sense in some places and a lot in others.

At last the day came when Anansi
collected what he felt sure was the very last
piece of common sense in the world. He
stuffed it into the calabash with
glee and clapped the top
back on.

'There! Now all I need to do is find a secret place to keep my precious treasure,' Anansi thought, looking around eagerly. His eyes fell on a very tall, very slender tree. "Perfect," he breathed, squinting up at the very top.

Anansi fetched a length of thick rope and attached both ends of it to the enormous calabash. Then he knotted the rope around his neck so the calabash dangled in front of him like a giant locket on a necklace. How uncomfortable it was! The rope cut into Anansi's neck and the calabash bashed into his stomach at his every move. Nevertheless, Anansi began determinedly to climb the tree.

Oof! It was hard work. Anansi was far

from his usual nimble self, with the big bulky calabash between himself and the tree. His fingers scrabbled to keep hold, his many legs trembled with the strain, his stomach ached with the bruising weight of the calabash pressed against it, and his neck burned from the rope.

Still, Anansi tried to keep his mind on being powerful and rich… and huffing and puffing, slipping and gripping, humping and bumping, up he went, little by little.

Anansi had climbed just over halfway up the tree when he heard someone giggling below him. He looked down and saw a young girl peering up at him.

"Oi! What are you laughing at?" Anansi shouted angrily.

"You!" sniggered the little girl. "Why on earth are you trying to climb with that calabash in front of you? If you had hung it behind you, so it dangled down your back, it would have been so much easier!"

Anansi couldn't believe his ears. How could he have missed that piece of common sense? If he'd missed that piece, how many more pieces had he missed? The thought filled Anansi with fury and frustration, and he lost his temper completely.

"Aaaaiiiiieeeee!" he screeched in a rage. He tore the rope from around his neck, and with all his might, threw the calabash away from him. Down… down… down it fell…

Crash! It hit the ground with an almighty thud and shattered. The pieces of common

sense spilled out, and were caught up by the wind and blown all over the world. That is why, today, there is common sense everywhere, for us all to share.

Mouse Deer and Tiger

A Southeast Asian folk tale

Mouse deer are common in South and Southeast Asian rainforests. A mouse deer is slightly larger than a domestic cat. Its legs and tail are like a deer's, but its face resembles that of a mouse. It features in many folk tales as a very cunning creature.

Once upon a time, there lived a cunning mouse deer in a big rainforest. He was so sharp-witted that all the other animals in the rainforest used to come to him with their problems, asking for his advice. So the mouse deer had many friends. However, he

also had some enemies. His worst enemy
was the ever-hungry tiger.

One day, the mouse deer was snoozing
in the shade under his favourite tree when
the tiger came stalking silently by, hunting
for food. The tiger had not eaten for many
days and his stomach was on fire. His eyes
lit up when he saw the sleeping little mouse
deer – he could hardly believe his luck.
Awake, the mouse deer was very fleet of
foot and extremely difficult to catch. He
was also silver-tongued and had tricked
him more times than the tiger cared to
remember. But now, the tiger could almost
taste the delicious morsel waiting for him.

He licked his lips – but the very light
smack of his tongue against his teeth was

all it took to wake the sharp-eared mouse deer. The little animal sprang up, instantly alert. He started in fright at the sight of the tiger's golden eyes, staring out at him from the undergrowth, and he leapt away at once. With a roar of frustration, the tiger made a mighty pounce and just managed to grab hold of the mouse deer's hoof.

"Aha! Now at last I have you!" the tiger growled delightedly. "And don't even think about trying to talk me out of eating you. You've conned me with your tall tales a million times before and I am not going to fall for your trickery again!"

"Fair enough," said the little mouse deer coolly, although inside he was trembling with fear. "But I'm warning you, once you've eaten me, don't even consider tasting that delicious cake over there." The mouse deer indicated a brown, roughly circular mound nearby, which he well knew was really a pile of monkey poo that had become mixed with some dried leaves. "That is a special cake that belongs to the king himself," the mouse deer continued.

"He ordered me to guard it and not let any animals in the forest taste it."

"But you weren't guarding it, you were sleeping," snarled the tiger gleefully. "I think I might go and tell the king, so he can punish you before I eat you."

"Oh, Mr Tiger, please don't do that," the mouse deer begged. "I'll tell you what, if you don't tell the king that I was sleeping, I will let you try the cake – just a teeny weeny bit. It must really be delicious if the king wants to keep it all to himself."

The tiger's stomach growled and he eyed the special cake greedily.

"Just let me walk a few steps away to the river over there," urged the mouse deer. "Then if the king's guards happen to pass by while you're tasting the cake, I can tell them that I was dying of thirst and really had to go for a drink – and perhaps the king will excuse me."

"Um – alright, I suppose so…" said the tiger, whose brain was befuddled by thoughts of the delicious cake. He released the mouse deer's hoof and the little creature ran away as fast as he could.

Of course, as soon as the tiger bit into the 'cake' he knew at once he had been tricked. "BLEUUURGH!" he yelled, spitting out the mouthful. Howling with rage, he sprang away into the rainforest after the mouse deer.

The tiger screeched to a halt when he found the little creature standing next to a wasps' nest. "Now, don't go telling me that's the king's new hat," snarled the tiger. "That's a wasps' nest, I know it is, so don't bother trying to fool me."

To the tiger's surprise, the mouse deer gave a little giggle. "The king's new hat!" he chuckled. "Anyone can see it's not the king's new hat. But you can't seriously think it's a wasps' nest." The mouse deer lowered his voice and whispered secretively, "Don't go telling anyone now – it's the king's new drum."

"The king's new drum? It doesn't look like one," answered the tiger uncertainly.

"That's because it's a special new kind of drum – the king doesn't want anyone to have one but him," announced the mouse deer. "The king doesn't even want anyone else to play this one," he continued, "but… I suppose it wouldn't hurt to let you have just one go, Tiger, to prove to you that it really is a drum."

"I agree," said the foolish tiger, "you've tricked me so many times that I refuse to believe this really is the king's new drum until I beat it for myself."

"Very well," replied the little mouse deer, "but I don't like the sound. It's much too loud for my sensitive ears. Let me stand among those trees over there."

"Alright," said the tiger, picking up a nearby stick.

Of course, the moment that the tiger hit the 'drum', wasps came buzzing out in an angry swarm and began stinging him all over. "OW! OW! OW!" screeched the tiger, running away as fast as he could to escape the furious insects.

In fact, he ran so fast and so far that the cunning little mouse deer never saw him in that part of the rainforest again.

The Reluctant Dragon

Adapted from the story by Kenneth Grahame

One evening long ago, a little shepherd boy was driving his flock home across the wide green ocean of the hills when he came across a dragon, lying half out of a cave. The dragon was as big as four carthorses and covered with shiny blue scales. As he breathed, little flames flickered up over his nostrils. He had his chin on his paws and appeared to be enjoying the cool of the evening. He was even purring!

The boy had read lots of fairy stories and knew all about dragons, so he wasn't afraid. "Hello dragon," he said – quietly, so as not to surprise the monster.

The dragon made to rise politely, but when he saw it was a boy he said severely: "Now don't you start throwing stones at me, or squirting water, or anything. I won't have it!"

"I'm not going to," said the boy, dropping onto the grass beside the beast. "I was just wondering how you were. But if I'm disturbing you, I can easily clear off."

"No, please don't go off in a huff,"

replied the dragon hastily. "I've not been here long – I do like it, but the fact is, it's a trifle dull at times."

The boy chewed on a stalk of grass. "Going to stay?" he inquired.

"I can't say," replied the dragon thoughtfully. "I am confoundedly lazy! The other fellows are always rampaging and skirmishing and chasing knights and devouring damsels. All I want is a meal and a snooze now and then, and plenty of time to think up poetry. On the whole, I feel quite inclined to settle down here…"

"The only problem being," said the boy, "that you're an enemy of the human race."

"I haven't got an enemy in the world," said the dragon. "Too lazy to make them!"

The Reluctant Dragon

"Oh dear," sighed the boy. "Listen – when other people find out you're here, they'll come after you with spears and swords. According to their thinking, you're a baneful monster!"

"Not a word of truth in it," said the dragon, wagging his head solemnly. "Now, do you want to hear that sonnet I was composing when you arrived?"

"If you won't be sensible," said the boy, getting up, "I'm off home. I'll look you up tomorrow. In the meantime, do try and realize that you're a pestilential scourge and you should leave, or you'll find yourself in a most awful fix. Goodnight!"

After that, the boy spent many a pleasant evening sitting with the dragon,

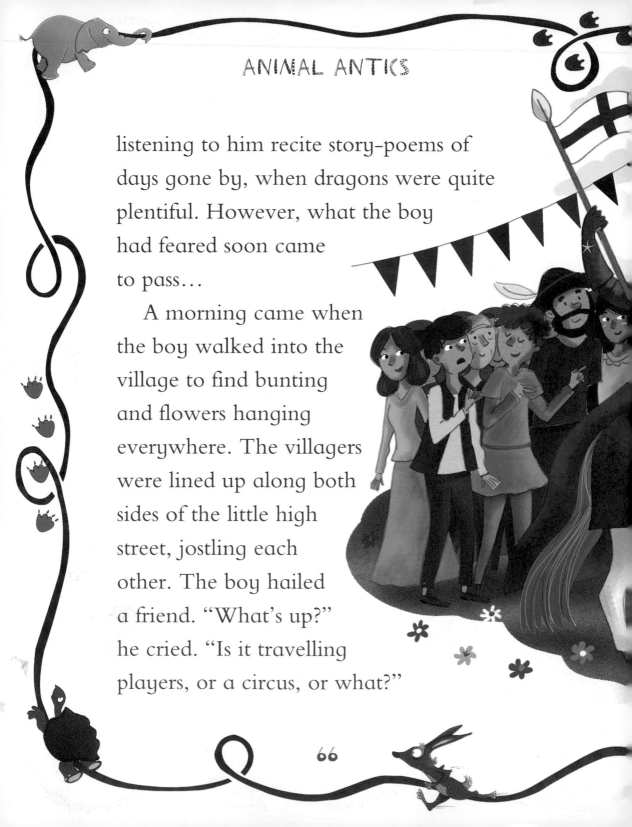

listening to him recite story-poems of days gone by, when dragons were quite plentiful. However, what the boy had feared soon came to pass…

A morning came when the boy walked into the village to find bunting and flowers hanging everywhere. The villagers were lined up along both sides of the little high street, jostling each other. The boy hailed a friend. "What's up?" he cried. "Is it travelling players, or a circus, or what?"

"Haven't you heard? There's a real live dragon in a cave in the hills!" replied his friend. "St George is coming to slay the deadly beast!"

Just then cheering broke out as a great warhorse pranced down the street, carrying St George in gleaming golden armour. The saint halted his horse in front of the inn, assured the cheering villagers that all would be well, then dismounted and strode confidently inside.

The boy made off up the hill as fast as he could go.

"The game's up, dragon!" he shouted as soon as he was within sight of the beast. "St George is here, and he's got the longest, wickedest-looking spear you ever did see!"

"Oh deary me," moaned the dragon. "You must tell him to go away. He can write if he likes, but I can't give him an interview. No offence to him – I'm not seeing anybody at present."

"Now dragon," implored the boy, "you've got to fight him, 'cos he's St George and you're the dragon. Better get it over with, and then we can go on with the story-poems."

"My dear little man," said the dragon solemnly, "I've never fought in my life and I'm not going to begin now. Just run down and make it alright, there's a dear chap."

So the boy rushed back to the village and burst into the inn, where St George was musing over his chances of winning.

"St George," panted the boy, "there's been a misunderstanding. This dragon is a good dragon. He's a friend of mine and tells the most beautiful story-poems."

"Draw up a chair," said St George. "I like a fellow who sticks up for his friends, and I'm sure the dragon has his good qualities. But are you absolutely certain there isn't some hapless princess tied up within yonder gloomy cavern?"

"I assure you, St George," the boy said earnestly, "there's nothing of the sort. The dragon's a real gentleman."

"Even if you're right," objected St George, "the rules say that the dragon and I have to fight."

"Well, why don't you at least meet the dragon for yourself and talk it over?" suggested the boy.

St George thought for a moment. "Well, it's irregular," he mused, "but it sounds sensible…" And off they strode together.

The dragon woke with a start as the pair approached.

"This is St George," introduced the boy. "St George, meet the dragon."

"So glad to meet you, St George,"

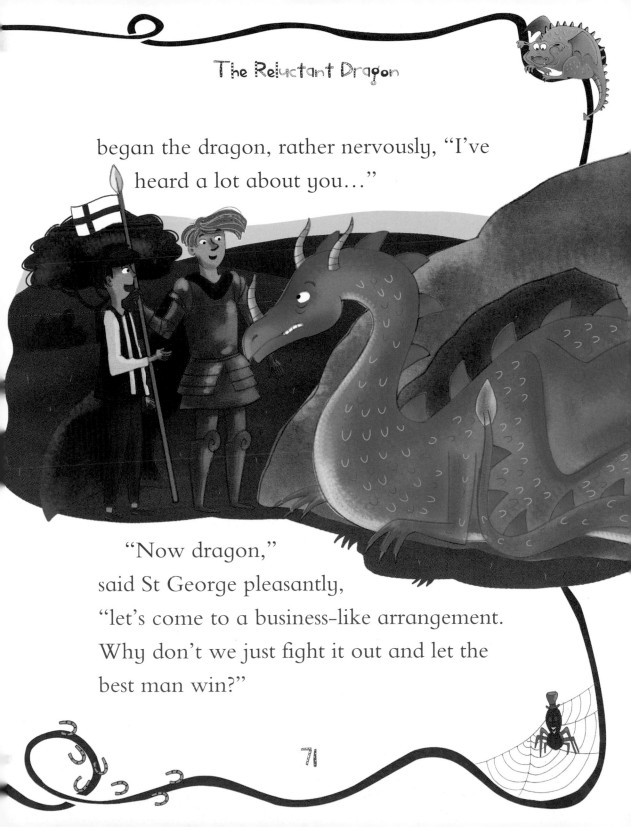

began the dragon, rather nervously, "I've heard a lot about you…"

"Now dragon," said St George pleasantly, "let's come to a business-like arrangement. Why don't we just fight it out and let the best man win?"

"But St George," the dragon protested, "the whole thing's nonsense. There's nothing to fight about. I'm simply not going to. If you try to make me, I shall just go into my cave and retire down a deep hole there until you get sick of sitting outside waiting for me."

St George gazed at the landscape around them. "But this would be such a beautiful place for a fight," he implored. "These great rolling hills for the arena, and me in my golden armour against your blue scaly coils! Think what a picture it would make!"

"Well, I suppose it would…" the imaginative dragon agreed, wavering.

"I could spear you somewhere it wouldn't hurt… under these folds of thick skin on your neck, for instance. You'd never even know I'd done it!" declared St George. "Then afterwards I'd lead you to the marketplace. I'd explain that you've seen the error of your ways, and so on. And then there would be the usual banquet."

"Well…" said the dragon, "I suppose I am bored up here, and I would indeed like to go into society. So…"

"Right, that's settled!" said the boy, winking at St George, who took the hint and rose to go.

"I'll even try to breathe fire," the dragon said. "It's surprising how easily one gets out of practice, but I'll do the best I can. Goodnight!"

Early next morning people began

streaming up into the hills in their Sunday clothes, carrying picnic baskets, intent on securing good places for the spectacle. The boy went to sit in the front, well up towards the cave, anxious that the dragon might change his mind and not show up.

Presently, cheering and the waving of handkerchiefs told the boy that St George was coming. Very gallant he looked on his warhorse, his golden armour glinting in the sun, his great spear held tall, its white flag with a red cross fluttering. St George halted his horse and then remained motionless, while the spectators watched in breathless expectation.

"Now then, dragon!" muttered the boy, fidgeting. But he needn't have worried.

The Reluctant Dragon

A low growling, mingled with snorts, rose to a bellowing roar. Then an impressive cloud of smoke obscured the mouth of the cave, and out of it the dragon came splendidly forth. "Ooooh!" everyone gasped. His blue scales glittered, his long spiky tail lashed, his claws tore up the turf, and smoke and fire shot from his nostrils.

"Oh, well done, dragon!" said the boy quietly to himself. "Didn't think he had it in him!"

With both contesters present, the battle began. St George lowered his spear, dug his heels into his horse's sides, and came thundering over the grass as the dragon charged with a roar. There was a moment's entanglement of golden armour with blue coils and spiky tail, and then the great horse, chomping at his bit, carried the saint clear.

"Incredible!" yelled the villagers.

'How well they managed that!' thought the boy.

St George steadied his horse and wiped his brow. Catching sight of the boy, he smiled and nodded. Then he hefted his spear and again galloped towards the dragon, who crouched at his approach, cracking his tail like a whip. The saint wheeled as he neared his opponent and the dragon rose onto his hind legs.

The end was so swift that all the boy saw was a mess of golden armour, spines, claws and flying turf. The dust cleared,

The Reluctant Dragon

the spectators cheered, and the boy saw that the dragon was pinned to the ground by the spear, St George astride him.

The boy ran towards them breathlessly, hoping the dear old dragon wasn't really hurt. As he approached, the dragon lifted one large eyelid, winked slowly and shut it again.

"Ain't you goin' to cut 'is 'ead off, master?" asked one of the applauding crowd. He had bet on the dragon to win, and naturally felt a trifle annoyed.

"There's no hurry," replied St George pleasantly. "Let's all go down to the village first and have some refreshment!"

He released the dragon, who rose and shook himself and ran his eye over his spikes and scales, to see that they were all in order. Then St George mounted his horse and led him away, in the company of the boy, with the cheering spectators following at a respectful distance behind.

Back in the village, everyone crowded round in front of the inn to hear St George give a speech. He told his audience that he had removed the source of their woe. That the dragon had been thinking things over and didn't want to be their enemy any more, but would like to stay and settle down. He told them that they must all make friends, and the villagers weren't to go thinking they'd got troubles, because they hadn't – besides, next time they'd have to do the fighting themselves.

Then he sat down, amid much cheering. The dragon nudged the boy in the ribs and whispered that he couldn't have said it better himself.

Finally, the banquet was prepared and the feasting began. What fun was had by all! St George was happy because there had been a fight and yet he hadn't had to kill anybody. The dragon proved to be delightful company and was the life and soul of the party. And the boy was happy because his two friends were on the best of terms, and all the villagers were happy too.

As midnight approached, the guests began to drop away with many goodnights and congratulations and invitations, and the dragon wandered out into the street followed by the boy and the saint. The dragon gazed up at the stars. "Jolly night it's been," he murmured.

And they set off up the hill arm-in-arm, the dragon, the boy and the saint.

Henny-penny

Adapted from a traditional tale
told by Joseph Jacobs

One day Henny-penny was pecking at grain in the yard when – *whack!* An acorn fell and hit her upon the head. "Goodness gracious me!" said Henny-penny. "The sky's a-going to fall – I must go and tell the king." Henny-penny was not particularly clever.

So she went along, and she went along, and she went along till she met Cocky-locky. "Where are you going,

Henny-penny?" said Cocky-locky.

"Oh! I'm going to tell the king the sky's a-falling in," said Henny-penny.

"May I come?" said Cocky-locky.

"Certainly," said Henny-penny. So Henny-penny and Cocky-locky went to tell the king the sky was falling in.

They went along, and they went along, and they went along till they met Ducky-daddles. "Where are you going to, Henny-penny and Cocky-locky?" said Ducky-daddles.

"Oh! We're going to tell the king the sky's a-falling in," said Henny-penny and Cocky-locky.

"May I come?" said Ducky-daddles.

"Certainly," said Henny-penny and Cocky-locky. So Henny-penny, Cocky-locky and Ducky-daddles went to tell the king the sky was falling in.

So they went along, and they went along, and they went along till they met Goosey-poosey. "Where are you going to, Henny-penny, Cocky-locky and Ducky-daddles?" said Goosey-poosey.

"Oh! We're going to tell the king the sky's a-falling in," said Henny-penny and Cocky-locky and Ducky-daddles.

"May I come?" said Goosey-poosey.

"Certainly," said Henny-penny, Cocky-locky and Ducky-daddles. So Henny-penny, Cocky-locky, Ducky-daddles and Goosey-poosey went to tell the king the sky was falling in.

So they went along, and they went along, and they went along till they met Turkey-lurkey. "Where are you going, Henny-penny, Cocky-locky, Ducky-daddles and Goosey-poosey?" said Turkey-lurkey.

"Oh! We're going to tell the king the

sky's a-falling in," said Henny-penny, Cocky-locky, Ducky-daddles and Goosey-poosey.

"May I come, Henny-penny, Cocky-locky, Ducky-daddles and Goosey-poosey?" said Turkey-lurkey.

"Why, certainly," said Henny-penny, Cocky-locky, Ducky-daddles and Goosey-poosey. So Henny-penny, Cocky-locky, Ducky-daddles, Goosey-poosey and Turkey-lurkey all went to tell the king the sky was falling in.

So they went along, and they went along, and they went along till they met Foxy-woxy. And Foxy-woxy said to Henny-penny, Cocky-locky, Ducky-daddles, Goosey-poosey and

Turkey-lurkey: "Where are you going, Henny-penny, Cocky-locky, Ducky-daddles, Goosey-poosey and Turkey-lurkey?"

"We're going to tell the king the sky's a-falling in," said Henny-penny, Cocky-locky, Ducky-daddles, Goosey-poosey and Turkey-lurkey.

"Oh! But this is not the way to the king, Henny-penny, Cocky-locky, Ducky-daddles, Goosey-poosey and Turkey-lurkey," said Foxy-woxy. "I know the right way, shall I show you?"

"Why certainly, Foxy-woxy," said Henny-penny, Cocky-locky, Ducky-daddles, Goosey-poosey and Turkey-lurkey. So Henny-penny, Cocky-locky,

Ducky-daddles, Goosey-poosey, Turkey-lurkey and Foxy-woxy all went to tell the king the sky was falling in.

So they went along, and they went along, and they went along till they came to a dark, narrow hole. This was the entrance to Foxy-woxy's cave.

But Foxy-woxy said to

Henny-penny, Cocky-locky, Ducky-daddles, Goosey-poosey and Turkey-lurkey: "This is the short cut to the king's palace — you'll soon get there if you follow me. I will go first and you come after, Henny-penny, Cocky-locky, Ducky-daddles, Goosey-poosey and Turkey-lurkey."

"Why of course, certainly, why not?" said Henny-Penny, Cocky-locky, Ducky-daddles, Goosey-poosey and Turkey-lurkey.

So Foxy-woxy went into his cave. He didn't go very far, but turned round to wait for Henny-Penny, Cocky-locky, Ducky-daddles, Goosey-poosey and Turkey-lurkey.

The Purple Gorilla

A North American traditional tale

A boy was cycling down a rough lane through the grassy, treeless prairie where he lived when he saw a turn-off that he hadn't noticed before. Being a curious child with a desire for excitement and adventure, he thought he would take a little detour on his way home and investigate, to see where it led.

No sooner had the boy cycled a little way down the track than the sky began to darken overhead. Heavy black clouds gathered — a storm was coming. As luck would have it, just as the first fat drops of rain began to fall, the boy spotted a house in the distance. He cycled as fast as he could, thinking he would shelter outside on the porch until the storm passed.

As the boy reached the house — *boom!* — the first clap of thunder crashed overhead. He dragged his bike up the steps of the porch and took a moment to catch his breath as the rain came hammering down. When he had recovered himself, he noticed a sign over the front door. In big black letters, it said:

WELCOME — COME ON IN

'That's strange,' thought the boy warily. But his curiosity got the better of him. He tried the door and found it unlocked. So he pushed it open, rather nervously – *creeeeak!* – and stepped inside.

The boy found himself in an ordinary-looking hallway. A coat and umbrella stand stood in the corner, pictures and a mirror hung on the walls, and there were several doors leading off. But it was the door directly ahead, at the far end of the hall, that caught the boy's attention. The door was not wooden like the others but made of heavy steel, and three big metal bolts were keeping it firmly locked. There was another sign on it, which in big black letters read:

The Purple Gorilla

KEEP
OUT

'That looks dangerous,' thought the boy.
But his curiosity got the better of him. He
crept down the hallway to the steel door,
and used both hands to heave back the
bolts – *thunk, thunk, thunk* – and push the
heavy metal door open – *screeeech!*

Behind the door, a staircase led downwards. 'Now that's just plain creepy,' thought the boy with a shudder. But his curiosity got the better of him. He stepped gingerly onto the first shadowy stair and carefully continued downwards – *squeak, squeak, squeak, squeak!*

At the bottom of the stairs was another sturdy metal door. This one was locked with a bulky chain and enormous padlock – although the key hung on the wall nearby. Another large sign warned:

TURN BACK NOW!
YES, THIS MEANS YOU!

'Me? Really?' thought the boy. But his curiosity got the better of him. He grabbed the key, thrust it into the padlock and turned it hard. It released with a loud and resounding *clunk!*

The boy pulled the door open – *eeeeep* – and stepped into a great big room. In the middle of the great big room there was a great big cage. And in the middle of the great big cage there was a great big purple gorilla. The great big purple gorilla was sitting on a stool with his legs crossed and his arms folded, looking awfully fed up.

DO NOT TOUCH
THE GORILLA!

cautioned an enormous sign hanging over the great big cage.

YOU CAN FEED HIM!
YOU CAN TALK TO HIM!
BUT WHATEVER YOU DO,
DO NOT TOUCH THE GORILLA!
YOU HAVE BEEN WARNED!

'Hmmm…' thought the boy, and his curiosity got the better of him.

A heap of bananas lay in the corner of the room. The boy picked one up and held it out between the bars. To his great surprise, the purple gorilla didn't jump up and snatch it, he reached

out one arm and took it quite lazily. He
peeled it precisely and ate it in several
dainty mouthfuls, almost as if he was doing
it out of politeness. Then, with a heavy
sigh, he folded his arms, still and bored
once more.

'Well, feeding him wasn't so
bad,' thought the boy, letting
his curiosity get the better of
him. 'Maybe I'll try talking
to him.' So the boy said:
"Hello, purple gorilla.
You do look down.
How long have you
been here? And why
do they keep you

you behind all these locked doors? What would actually happen if I touched you?"

The boy didn't really expect the purple gorilla to talk back – and of course, he didn't. He just sat there on his stool with his legs crossed and his arms folded, gazing into the distance as if he couldn't hear a word.

Feeling bolder, the boy giggled naughtily and jigged about in front of the cage, pulling a face. But the purple gorilla took no notice at all.

"I wonder…" the boy murmured to himself. He stepped right up close to the bars and thrust his arm through. The purple gorilla didn't even look at him. So the boy raised himself up on tiptoe, pressed himself right up against the bars, reached out at absolute full stretch – and his fingertips just touched the gorilla.

Quick as a flash, the purple gorilla sprang to his feet with a mighty howl and grabbed the bars of his cage. The boy screamed fit to burst. The gorilla began to bend the bars apart with all his might.

The boy didn't wait to see any more. With his heart pounding, he span round and raced for the door.

TOLD YOU SO!

mocked a sign over the door frame as he sped through.

Squeak! Squeak! Squeak! Squeak! The boy took the stairs two at a time as he heard from behind him an almighty *crash!* The purple gorilla had broken the cage apart!

The boy sped back through the steel door, where a sign hanging above it read:

> BET YOU WISH NOW YOU HADN'T TOUCHED THE GORILLA!

The boy tore down the hallway, the floor shaking beneath his feet. He glanced over his shoulder to see the purple gorilla striding through the steel door behind him – *thump, thump, thump, thump!*

By the front door, the boy spotted a sign informing him:

> THIS IS YOUR OWN FAULT, YOU KNOW!

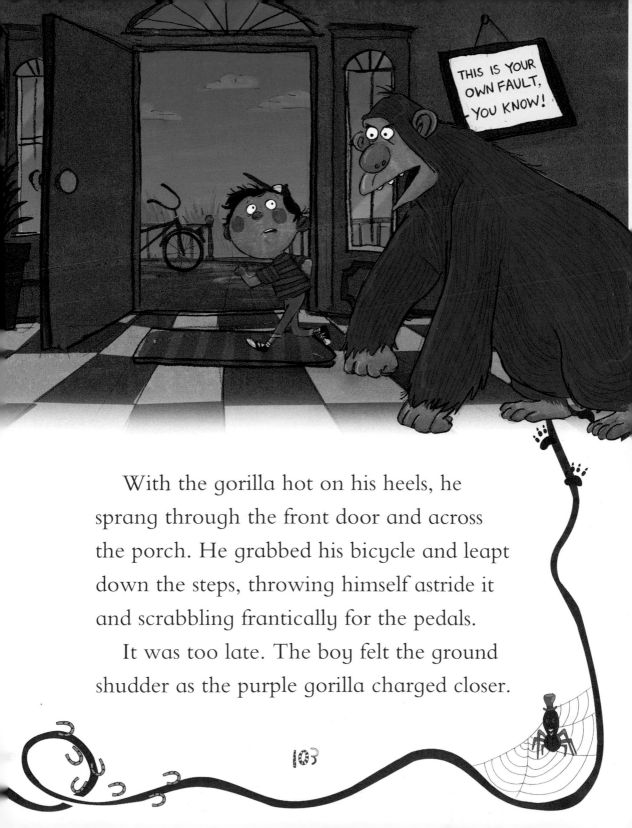

THIS IS YOUR
OWN FAULT,
YOU KNOW!

With the gorilla hot on his heels, he
sprang through the front door and across
the porch. He grabbed his bicycle and leapt
down the steps, throwing himself astride it
and scrabbling frantically for the pedals.

It was too late. The boy felt the ground
shudder as the purple gorilla charged closer.

Terrified, the boy looked round.

There was the great big purple gorilla standing right behind him. The gorilla reached out his great big hand…

…with his great big fingers…

…and touched the boy lightly on the shoulder. "Tag. You're it," said the gorilla with a grin.

The Man and his Camel

Adapted from a Middle Eastern traditional tale
retold by Horace E Scudder

One cold night, hundreds of years ago, a desert-dweller sat in his tent. He was greatly surprised when a camel thrust the tent flap aside and peered in.

"I beg you, Master," he said, "let me put my head within the tent, for it is so cold here outside under the stars."

"Be my guest," said the desert-dweller. So the camel poked his head into the tent.

The two stayed like that in companionable silence for a while, before the camel politely inquired, "Master, would you be so kind as to allow me to warm my neck also?"

"Of course, do indeed put your neck inside," said the man, so the camel gratefully moved further into the tent.

However, he soon began turning his head from side to side and wriggling uncomfortably. "Master," said the camel, "I don't think it would take up much more room if I put my forelegs inside the tent. It is quite a strain to stretch only my neck inside."

The man nodded graciously. "You may also put your forelegs inside," he said, shifting over a little to make room, for the tent was very small.

But after a while, the camel sighed noisily and said: "Perhaps it would be best

if I stood entirely inside the tent? After all, by standing half-in and half-out like this, I'm keeping the tent flap open and the chill

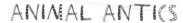

night air is blowing in."

"Yes, yes," said the man. "There's no need for us both to freeze. Why don't you come wholly inside?"

So the camel moved forward until his whole body was inside the tent. His head pushed up against the roof, straining the fabric, and his flanks pressed against the man, so there was not enough space for either of them to even scratch an itch.

"I think," resolved the camel, "that there is not room for both of us in here. It will be best if you stand outside, as you are the smaller of us – there will then be sufficient space for me."

And with that he gave the man a shove, sending him tumbling through the tent flap.

The Man and his Camel

The desert-dweller found himself outside in the freezing desert night, wondering how on earth he had come to end up there…

Fantastic Fools

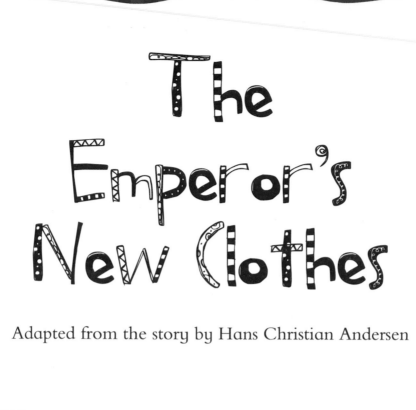

The Emperor's New Clothes

Adapted from the story by Hans Christian Andersen

There was once an emperor who loved new clothes above everything else. Designers, tailors, cloth-makers, dyers, and specialists in all sorts of needlework travelled to his city from all over the world. Anyone who could create flashy, fancy new outfits for the emperor was always very welcome at the palace.

One day, it was the turn of two weavers to be ushered into the emperor's dressing room. The emperor, his butler and all the Officers of the Royal Wardrobe listened in amazement as they described their work.

"We have created a special type of fabric so light and airy the wearer cannot even feel it is there," the first weaver announced proudly.

"Our samples are top secret, which is why we have not brought any to show you," the second weaver explained.

"However, we can assure you that not only are our designs and patterns exquisitely beautiful," continued the first weaver, "but the fabric has a unique advantage – it is completely invisible to anyone not worthy of his job—"

"—or just plain stupid!" laughed the second weaver, and the emperor and all his courtiers gasped and chuckled along.

"We would be truly honoured if you were to order the very first suit of clothes made out of this extraordinary fabric, Your Imperial Majesty," said the first weaver, bowing low.

The emperor clapped his hands with delight. "I'd like to place an order right away!" he declared, and he gave the two weavers a large sum of money so that they could buy the rare, expensive materials they needed and begin work without delay.

A room in the palace was set aside for the weavers. They set up their looms and got going right away. Meanwhile, news of the strange and incredible cloth spread round the city like wildfire, and soon everyone was talking about it. The weavers worked behind closed doors so no one got even a glimpse of what they were doing. Still, day and night the courtiers and servants in the palace could hear the looms clicking and the shuttles flying – work on the mysterious fabric seemed to be progressing well.

As the days went on, the emperor began

to feel rather uneasy about seeing the cloth for the first time. 'Imagine if I can't see it!' he thought. 'How dreadfully embarrassing that would be!' The worried emperor decided to send his trusted old butler to see how the weavers were getting on. He was sure that his butler was both fit for his job and very wise, and would definitely be able to see the wonderful material.

The weavers bowed low and ushered the butler in. But to the old man's horror, he couldn't see anything at all. 'Heavens above!' the butler thought to himself. 'Those looms look totally bare to me! I must either be a very bad butler, or else I'm an idiot. No one must ever find out…' So he praised the fabric that he could not see, told the emperor that the weavers' work was indeed magnificent, and in due course, everyone in the city heard that the cloth was truly unbelievable.

Soon afterwards, the weavers sent word to the emperor that they needed more money to buy essential items for the work. The emperor had been so delighted with his butler's report that he sent them twice as much money as before.

The emperor was more excited than ever. "I'm going to have the most amazing suit of clothes in the world!" he said to himself ten times a day.

Eventually, just as the impatient emperor thought he was going to explode with anticipation, the weavers announced their work was finished. They went to the dressing room to present the material to the emperor amid fanfares of trumpets. "Is the cloth not beautiful beyond all imagining?" the weavers sighed.

The emperor smiled a wide smile, trying to hide his horror. The weavers appeared to be holding up nothing but thin air before him. The emperor's worst fear had come true – to him the fabric was invisible!

'I cannot be thought to be a fool or an unworthy ruler,' the despairing emperor thought. So he beamed and leant forwards, inspecting the air between the weavers' hands. "Wonderful! Splendid! Magnificent!" he cried. His butler and all the Officers of the Royal Wardrobe nodded and joined him in calling out compliments. None of them could see anything either, but they weren't about to risk losing their jobs by admitting it.

So the weavers got out their tape measures and their scissors and they set about cutting the air (so it seemed) into a pattern. All night long they sewed with needles that appeared to have no thread, and in the morning they announced that the emperor's new clothes were ready. "Now if Your Imperial Majesty would care to disrobe, we will dress you in the amazing garments," they told him.

The emperor swallowed hard and took off all his clothes. The weavers helped him on with the underpants and trousers and shirt and jacket, all invisible to him. "How do they feel?" they asked him. "Lighter than air?" The emperor spluttered his agreement. He couldn't feel that he had any clothes on at all.

The emperor turned to the mirror. According to what he saw, he didn't have a stitch on! But he turned this way and that, pretending to admire himself. And the butler and all the Officers of the Royal Wardrobe keenly cried out, "How wonderfully the new clothes fit you, Your Majesty!" and "Such amazing colours!"

and "The design is a work of genius!" – even though it looked to all of them that the emperor was as naked as the day he was born.

'Everyone else can see my new suit except me,' the emperor thought, horrified. But, summoning his courage, he walked out of the palace to parade before the people in his marvellous new clothes.

The streets were lined with hundreds of people who *ooohed* and *aaahed* and applauded at the sight of the emperor's new clothes – for no one wanted to admit that they couldn't see them.

Suddenly, a shrill little voice rose above the noise of the crowd. "But the emperor has nothing on!" a young boy shouted.

"Nothing on at all!"

A stunned silence followed and the boy found hundreds of pairs of eyes staring at him. Then someone sniggered… someone else tried to stifle a giggle… another person let out a snort… and the whole crowd burst into uncontrollable laughter.

The emperor's face turned as red as a ripe tomato. "I am indeed a fool!" he cried. "I have been swindled by two tricksters!" He ran back to the palace as fast as his short, naked legs could carry him – but the clever (and now very rich) weavers were long gone!

The Thunder God Gets Married

A Norse myth

Up in heaven, Thor the thunder god was furious. Someone had stolen his magic hammer, Mijolnir. The hammer was the terror of the gods. Whenever Thor threw it, it killed anything that it touched and then always returned to his hand. Mijolnir was perhaps the most deadly weapon that the gods possessed to protect them against their enemies, the giants.

Now Thor's roars of rage sounded like the clouds were crashing together. His face was so dark with anger that it sent a shadow across the sky. As Thor grabbed blazing lightning bolts and hurled them through the clouds, the mischief-maker god, Loki, came nervously to see him.

"I have good news, my angry friend," Loki explained. "I have used my cunning to find out that it was the giant Thrym who stole your hammer. He has agreed to give it back on one condition – that he has the most beautiful of all the goddesses, Freya, as his bride."

The thunder god's sulky face brightened

a little. He charged off to find Freya straight away. "Put on your best dress, Freya!" Thor boomed, throwing open her wardrobe doors. "You have to marry the giant Thrym so I can get back Mijolnir."

Freya's eyes flickered with cold fire. "Excuse me," she said calmly. "Would you care to repeat that?"

"You-have-to-marry-the-giant-Thrym-so-I-can-get-back-Mijolnir!" the impatient thunder god cried, the words flying from his mouth at top speed.

Freya stood glaring, her hands on her hips. "Firstly, Thor, I don't *have* to do anything."

Thor's face reddened.

"Secondly," Freya continued, "I wouldn't marry that ugly giant if he were the only creature left in the world."

The thunder god hung his head.

"Thirdly," Freya declared, "it's your problem, so you sort it out."

"Sorry, Freya," Thor mumbled, shuffling about a bit. Then he turned and stormed back to Loki. The two gods sat down glumly and wracked their brains to come up with another way to get the magic hammer back.

"How about…" Thor started to suggest. Then he shook his head. "No, no good."

"What if…" Loki began. Then his face fell. "No, it would never work."

It looked as if Mijolnir would have to stay in the land of the giants forever – until the god Heimdall had an idea.

"That's absolutely out of the question!" Thor thundered on hearing it.

"Outrageous!" Loki squealed. "I'll never do it!"

"Well, you come up with another plan then," Heimdall laughed, knowing that there wasn't one.

That afternoon, there was great

merriment among the gods and goddesses as they dressed Thor up like a beautiful maiden. How they laughed as they brushed and curled the thunder god's fair hair, and set a coronet of silver and pearls upon his head. They taunted and teased Thor as they adjusted a shimmering gown of Freya's for him to wear, letting out seams and lowering hems, lengthening sleeves and setting in extra panels to make it larger – much larger, for Thor insisted on keeping his chain mail shirt and belt of power on underneath it.

Then finally they draped over the coronet a veil that covered Thor's face. And there the thunder god stood, as beautiful a bride as a giant might wish for.

"I don't know why you're laughing," the furious Thor said to a giggling Loki. "It's your turn next."

And the horrified Loki was given similar treatment by the gods and goddesses until he looked like the perfect bridesmaid for the perfect bride.

As dusk fell that evening, the giant Thrym was delighted to see a chariot with a bride and bridesmaid in it arriving at the castle steps.

"It's Freya!" the gormless giant gasped with delight, as the two figures clambered out. "I shall gladly give back Thor's precious Mijolnir in return for the most beautiful wife in the world!" The overjoyed giant ordered a magnificent wedding

banquet to be prepared and his guests to be
sent for at once.

But Thrym wouldn't have been so
happy if he could have seen beneath the
veils of the bride and bridesmaid, and the
angry, highly embarrassed faces of Thor

and Loki. As it was, the giant was far too excited – and stupid – to notice how big and clumsy the bride and bridesmaid looked in their delicate dresses. Thrym didn't take in that the women had low, gruff voices and huge hands. And he hardly thought twice about the way that Freya swigged down two whole barrels of beer and devoured an entire roast ox.

When all the guests had eaten and drunk their fill, the beaming Thrym got to his feet to make a speech. "My wife and I," he began, "would like to thank you all for coming here today to celebrate this happy occasion with us. Freya has made me the luckiest being in heaven and Earth. And now, I will keep my word and give back the magic hammer I stole from that ugly thug of a thunder god."

There was a drum roll as one of Thrym's servants brought in Mijolnir on a velvet cushion. Thrym held it high in the air for his marvelling guests to admire, then with a grand flourish, he presented it to his bride.

"The ugly thug of a thunder god thanks you!" roared Thor, ripping off his veil and springing to his feet. He seized the hammer, and before the dismayed Thrym and his guests could really take in the trick, Thor and Loki had disappeared, and the wedding feast was unexpectedly over.

All the gods were truly relieved to have the magic hammer back in Thor's hands in heaven, where it belonged. But it was a long time before Thor and Loki could laugh with the other gods about how charming they both looked in a dress!

Hans in Luck

Adapted from a traditional tale
by the Brothers Grimm

Once upon a time, there was a young man named Hans who always considered himself to be lucky. He was hard-working too. He laboured for a wealthy man for seven long years, at the end of which the man said, "You have been a faithful and good servant, Hans." And he gave Hans a big lump of silver.

Hans wrapped the piece of silver in his handkerchief, threw it over his shoulder and

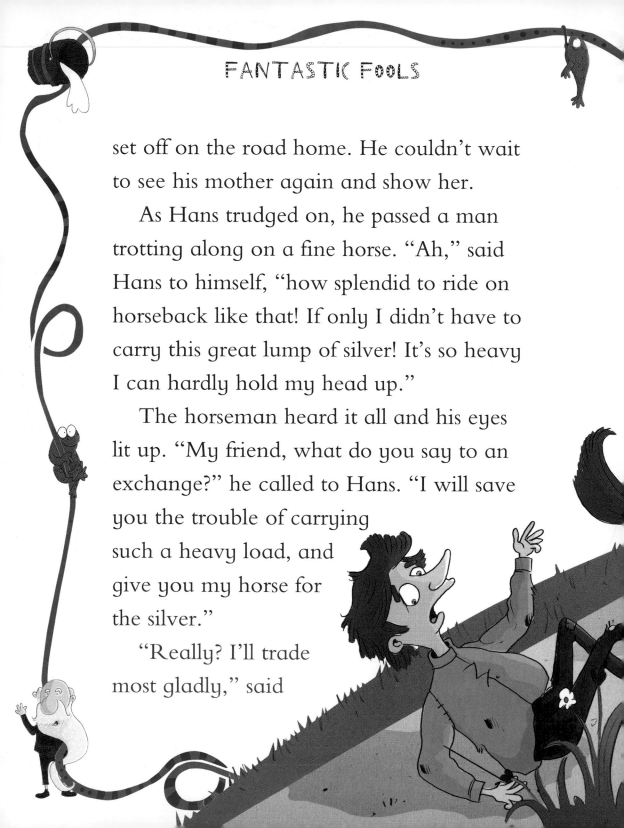

set off on the road home. He couldn't wait to see his mother again and show her.

As Hans trudged on, he passed a man trotting along on a fine horse. "Ah," said Hans to himself, "how splendid to ride on horseback like that! If only I didn't have to carry this great lump of silver! It's so heavy I can hardly hold my head up."

The horseman heard it all and his eyes lit up. "My friend, what do you say to an exchange?" he called to Hans. "I will save you the trouble of carrying such a heavy load, and give you my horse for the silver."

"Really? I'll trade most gladly," said

Hans, unable to believe his luck.

So the horseman got off and took the silver, then helped Hans onto the horse and handed him the reins. Hans was extremely pleased and rode off whistling cheerily.

After a time Hans thought he should like to go a little faster, so he cried "Jip!" Away went the horse at full gallop and Hans found himself thrown off. He landed heavily by the roadside. His horse would have run off, if a drover who was coming by with a cow had not stopped it.

137

Hans picked himself up, most dismayed, and said to the drover, "This riding business is no joke – I could have broken my neck! Your cow is much better than this horse. After all, one can stroll along behind a cow – and she'd give you milk, butter and cheese every day, into the bargain."

"Well," said the drover, "just to help you out I will exchange my cow for your horse, if you like."

"Done!" said Hans merrily. So the drover climbed up onto the horse and away he rode.

Hans continued on, walking his cow towards his mother's village. As noon approached and the heat grew greater, he decided to milk the cow and quench his thirst. So he tied her to a tree trunk and placed a discarded pail underneath her – but not a drop was to be had! Hans hadn't considered that this cow might be old and past milking.

Just then the uneasy beast grew tired of being bothered and pushed Hans over into a puddle. As luck would have it, a butcher was passing by pushing a pig in a wheelbarrow, and helped Hans up.

"If only my old cow were a pig like yours," sighed Hans. "I may not have milk, but at least I would have sausages."

"Well," said the butcher, "to do a neighbourly thing, I will give you my fine fat pig for your cow."

"May heaven reward you for your

135

kindness!" said Hans, as he gave the butcher the cow and took the pig.

And on Hans went – until he met a farmer carrying a fine white goose. Hans told the farmer all about his luck and how he had made so many good bargains.

The farmer looked at the pig and sucked in his breath. "I hate to say this, my friend," he said, "but in the village I just came from, the squire has had a pig stolen from his sty. I can't help thinking that's the squire's pig. If it is, and they catch you, the least they will do is throw you into the river. Can you swim?"

"No," cried Hans, very frightened.

"I'll tell you what," said the farmer, "I'll do you a huge favour and take that pig off

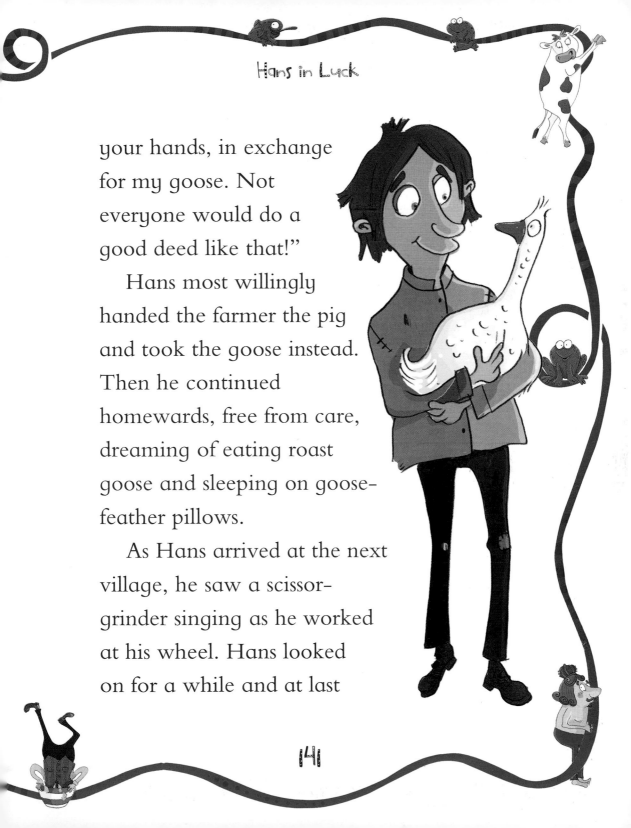

your hands, in exchange for my goose. Not everyone would do a good deed like that!"

Hans most willingly handed the farmer the pig and took the goose instead. Then he continued homewards, free from care, dreaming of eating roast goose and sleeping on goose-feather pillows.

As Hans arrived at the next village, he saw a scissor-grinder singing as he worked at his wheel. Hans looked on for a while and at last said, "You seem very happy, sir!"

"Yes," said the scissor-grinder, "I am very well paid for my work. A good grinder never puts his hand into his pocket without finding money in it… but where did you get that beautiful goose?"

"I did not buy it," explained Hans, "I exchanged a pig for it."

"And where did you get the pig?" asked the grinder.

"I gave a cow for it," Hans told him.

"And the cow?" inquired the grinder.

"I gave a horse for it."

"And the horse?"

"I gave a lump of silver as big as my head for it."

"And the silver?"

"Oh! I worked hard for that for seven long years."

"Well, you have had good luck, haven't you?" said the grinder with a wry smile. "Now, if only you could find money in your pocket whenever you put your hand in it, your fortune would be made."

"Very true," agreed Hans, "but how do I manage that?"

"Why, you become a scissor-grinder like myself," replied the grinder. "In fact, I'll give you my grindstone. It's a little bit worse for wear, so I'll let you have it in exchange for your goose."

"I shall be the happiest man in the world to have money in my pocket whenever I put my hand in it," sighed Hans.

So the grinder gave him the rough, worn grindstone that lay by his side, took the plump goose and hurried away.

Hans continued on his way with a light heart. But after a little while he began to grow thirsty – and exhausted from carrying the stone. He dragged himself to the side of the river, to take

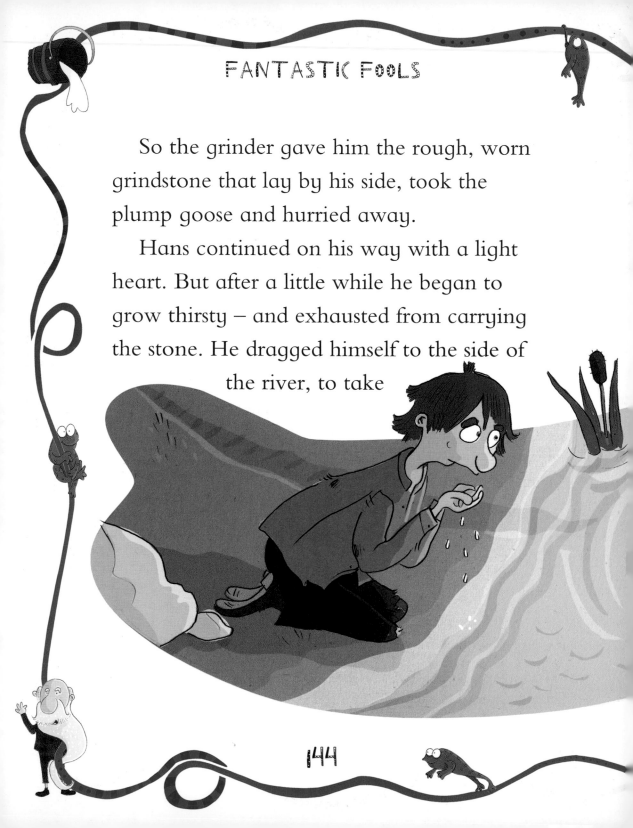

a drink of water and rest. He laid the stone carefully on the bank, but as he knelt to drink, he nudged it just a little and down it rolled, *plop* into the stream.

Hans watched it sink. Then suddenly he sprang up and danced for joy. "Thank you heaven," he cried, "for taking away my burden, that heavy stone!"

Then on he walked with a

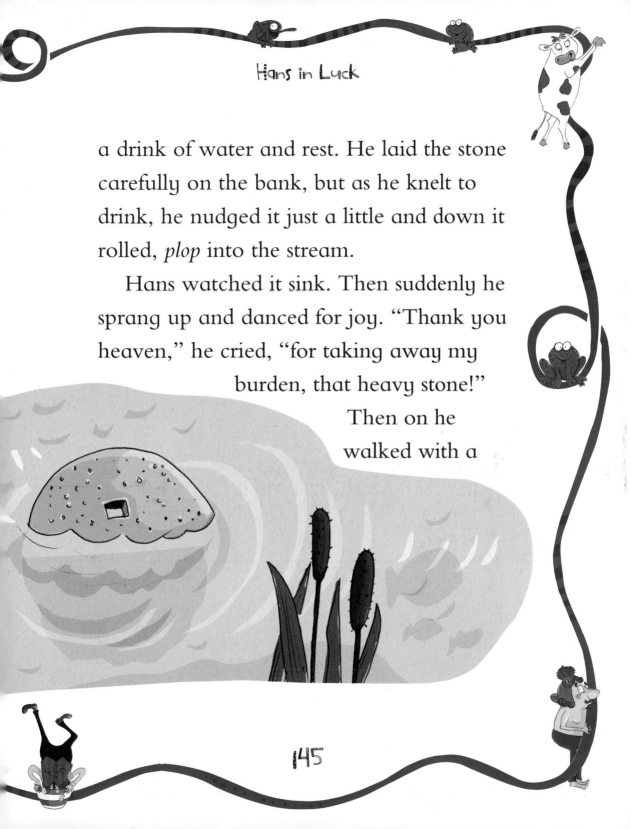

145

light heart, free from all his troubles, till he reached his mother's house and told her what a very lucky fellow he was.

The Dragon-tamers

Adapted from the story by E Nesbit

There was once an old, old castle, most of which had crumbled to ruins. Of all its past splendour there were only two little rooms left – and it was here that John the blacksmith had set up his forge. No one asked any rent for the rooms, because all the lords of the castle were dead and gone. So there John blew his bellows and hammered his iron and did all the work that came his way.

John kept his tools and coal in the great
dungeon underneath the castle. It was a
fine dungeon indeed, with a handsome
vaulted roof and iron rings for tying
prisoners to. At one end was a broken flight
of steps leading down to no one knew
where. John himself had never dared to go
beyond the seventh step…

One evening, John was busy at his forge
while his wife sat and nursed their baby.
Presently, over the noise of the bellows and
the clank of the iron, there came another
sound – like the noise of some great
creature purring, purring, purring down
below. John took his shovel in one hand
and his hammer in the other, hung the old
stable lantern on his little finger, and went

down the winding stairs to the dungeon.

Half of the dungeon was empty as usual, except for his tools and the coal. But the other side was not empty. It was quite full, and what it was full of was a dragon.

'It must have come up those broken steps from goodness knows where,' thought John, trembling all over, as he tried to creep back up the winding stairs.

But the dragon shot out a great claw and caught him by the leg. "No you don't," the beast said in a deep voice. "You're the very man I need. Some rivets have fallen out of one of my wings. Could you put that to rights?"

John timidly looked the dragon over. He seemed to be made almost entirely of iron armour – a sort of tawny, rusty colour it was – and under it he seemed to be covered in fur. Sure enough, his wing was loose.

"You could certainly do with a rivet or two, sir," said John politely. "In fact, you want a good many."

"Well, get to work, then," said the dragon. "You mend my wing, then I'll go and eat up all the town – and if you make a really smart job of it I'll eat you last!"

"Great," said John despairingly. "Would you just let me fasten you up, like I do with horses?"

"Fasten me up?" said the dragon. "How do I know you'd untie me again? Give me something in pledge. What do you value most?"

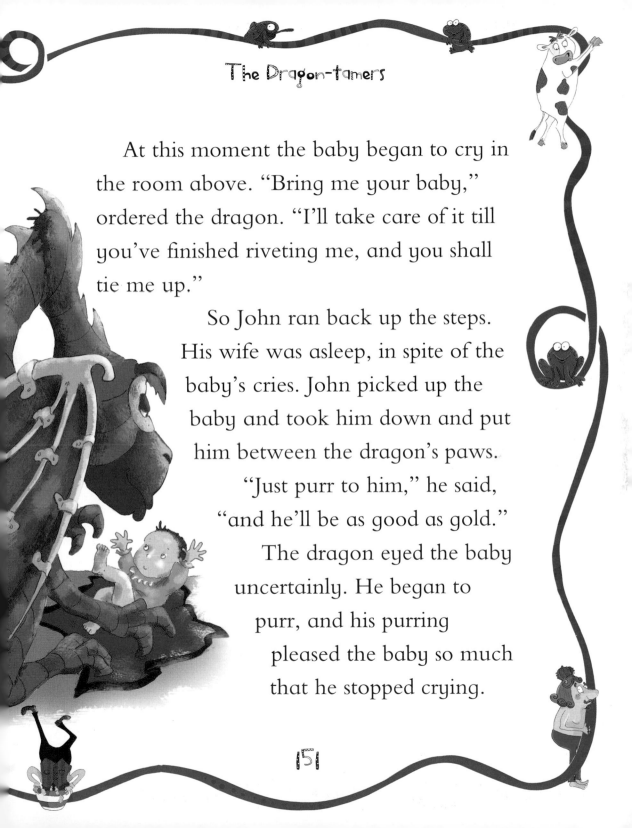

At this moment the baby began to cry in the room above. "Bring me your baby," ordered the dragon. "I'll take care of it till you've finished riveting me, and you shall tie me up."

So John ran back up the steps. His wife was asleep, in spite of the baby's cries. John picked up the baby and took him down and put him between the dragon's paws.

"Just purr to him," he said, "and he'll be as good as gold."

The dragon eyed the baby uncertainly. He began to purr, and his purring pleased the baby so much that he stopped crying.

Then John brought some heavy chains and a great collar that had been made in the days when men sang over their work and put their hearts into it. When he had safely locked the dragon up in them, he scratched his head and said: "Do you know, I don't think I have enough rivets in the shop. If you'll excuse me, I'll just step around to another forge and get a few dozen. I won't be a minute."

And off he went, leaving the baby between the dragon's forepaws, laughing and gurgling with pleasure at his purring.

John immediately ran upstairs, shook his wife awake and told her the tale.

"You've given the baby to the dragon!" she cried. "Oh, how could you!"

"Hush," he said, "I'm going back down. After I've been you can go, and if you keep your head the boy will be alright."

So back down the stairs went the blacksmith, and there was the dragon purring away to keep the baby quiet.

"Hurry up, can't you?" he said. "I can't keep up this noise all night."

"I'm very sorry, sir," replied John, "but all the shops are shut. The job must wait till the morning. And don't forget you've promised to take care of the baby. Goodnight, sir." And off he went up the stairs before the dragon could respond.

The dragon had purred till he was quite out of breath — so he stopped. As soon as he did so, the baby started to scream again.

"Oh, dear," said the dragon mournfully, "this is awful." He patted the baby with his claw, but the boy screamed more than ever. Looking around in panic, he noticed a woman sitting on the steps. "I say," he said, "do you know anything about babies?"

"I do, a little," said the woman.

"Then I beg you to take this one and let me get some sleep," implored the dragon, yawning and exposing his sharp teeth.

So John's wife picked up her baby and took him upstairs. She told John what had happened and they went to bed happy, for they had tricked the dragon.

After this, things went a little better for John. To begin with, the baby did not cry quite so much. On top of that, word of the dragon spread and tourists came from a long way off, paying twopence each to go down the steps and have a look at the rusty dragon in the dungeon.

The baby – named John, after his father – began presently to grow up. He was great friends with Tina, the daughter of the family who lived down the hill. Together, the children would go and peep into the dungeon at the dragon, and sometimes they would hear him mew piteously.

Then one day, people came running into town screaming that a giant was lumbering over the marshes towards them.

Johnnie and Tina looked at each other and then sped off as fast as their boots would carry them, up to the castle and down the dungeon steps. They went in and began to talk casually to the dragon, telling him what the weather was like outside, and what there was in the papers. At last, Johnnie said: "By the way, there's a giant in the town. He wants you."

"Does he really?" said the dragon, baring his teeth. "If only I were free, I'd show him!"

So the children unlocked the dragon from the chains and collar, and he broke down one end of the dungeon and went out – pausing only at the forge door to get John the blacksmith to fix his wing.

He met the giant at the town gate. The giant hit the dragon with his club, and the dragon replied with smoke and fire. It

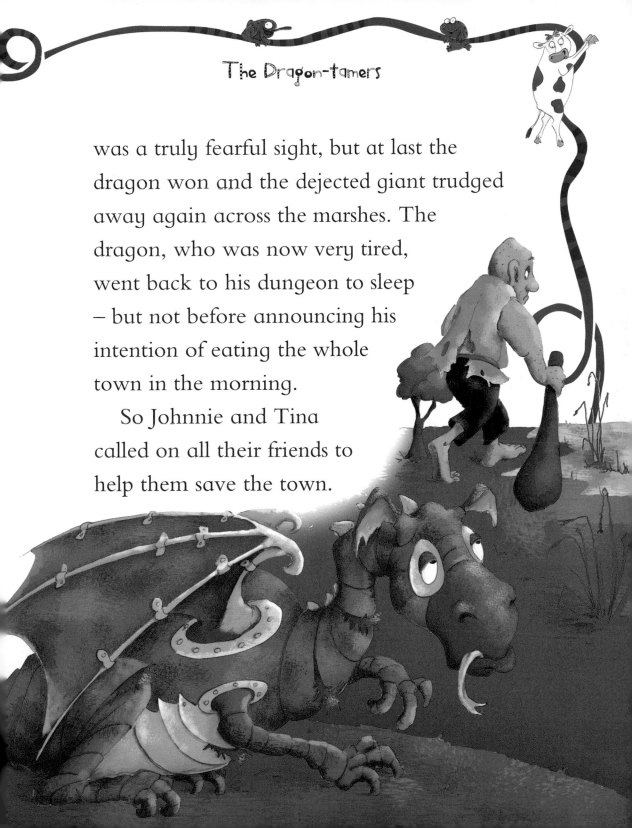

was a truly fearful sight, but at last the
dragon won and the dejected giant trudged
away again across the marshes. The
dragon, who was now very tired,
went back to his dungeon to sleep
– but not before announcing his
intention of eating the whole
town in the morning.

So Johnnie and Tina
called on all their friends to
help them save the town.

"You must all bring your breakfasts of bread and milk to the forge tomorrow morning," Johnnie and Tina said, and all the children promised.

Next morning, when all the children brought their bread and milk, Tina and Johnnie emptied it into a huge washtub. When the tub was full, with the help of nine other children they carried it down the dungeon steps and called out: "May we come in?"

"Oh, yes," said the dragon, "it's very dull here."

So they went in and set down the washtub next to the dragon. Then the other children went away, and Tina and Johnnie sat on the floor and pretended to cry, letting out big exaggerated sobs.

"What's this?" asked the dragon. "And what's the matter?"

"There's another giant!" wailed Johnnie. "He's so big he makes the first giant look like a dwarf."

"But he doesn't want to eat us," Tina went on. "He says he'll spare us if he can eat you – with bread sauce."

"That's unfortunate," said the dragon. "And I suppose this sloppy stuff in the tub is the bread sauce?"

The children said it was. "Of course," Johnnie added, "bread sauce is always served with wild dragons. You have to have apple sauce with tame ones, and this giant hates apple sauce. What a pity you're not a tame one – he'd never want to eat you then."

"Goodbye, poor dragon," said Tina, "this is the last time we will ever see you." And both children began to cry noisily once more.

"Well, look here," said the dragon, "couldn't you tell the giant I am actually a tame dragon you keep for a pet?"

"He'd never believe it," said Johnnie. "If you were a tame dragon you'd be kept tied up, you know."

Then the dragon begged them to fasten him up, and they did so at once and hurried off.

When the captive dragon realized that he'd been tricked, he began to weep. Then the poor creature dried his eyes and looked about him, and there he saw the tub of bread and milk. 'If giants like this damp, white stuff, perhaps I would like it too,' he thought, and he tasted a little, and liked it so much that he ate it all up.

And the next time tourists came, the dragon asked shyly: "Excuse my troubling you, but could you bring me a little more bread and milk?"

After that, people took the dragon bread and milk every day.

And so ten years passed. Johnnie became mayor, and he and Tina fell in love. On the morning of their wedding they went to see the dragon. He had grown quite tame. His rusty plates had fallen off in places, and underneath he was soft and furry to stroke. So they stroked him gently.

"I don't know how I could ever have liked eating anything but bread and milk," the dragon said wonderingly. "I am a tame dragon now, aren't I? Won't you undo me at last?"

And Johnnie and Tina were so happy on their wedding day that they unlocked the chains and collar.

As the dragon followed Johnnie and Tina out of the castle into sunshine, he blinked and shook himself. The last of his rusty plates dropped off, his wings with them, and all of a sudden he was just like a very, very oversized cat.

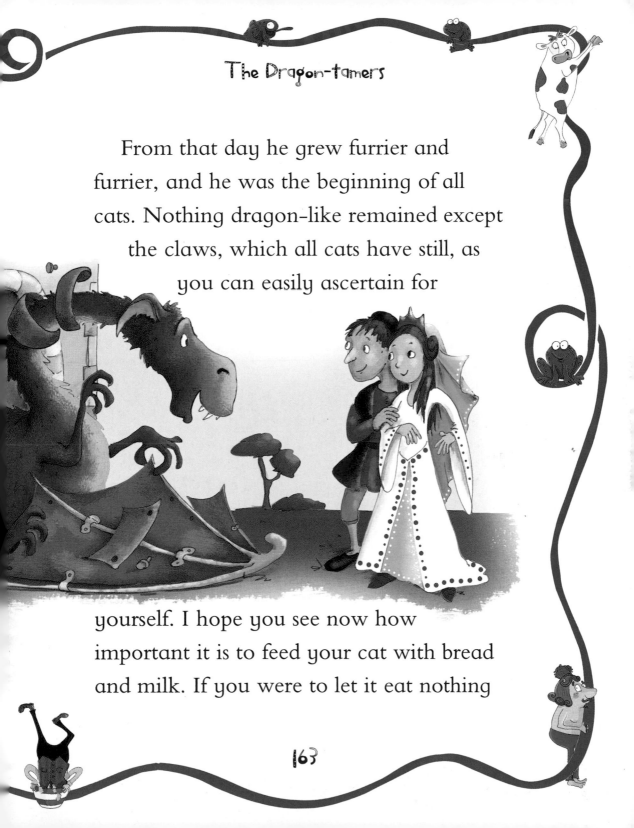

From that day he grew furrier and furrier, and he was the beginning of all cats. Nothing dragon-like remained except the claws, which all cats have still, as you can easily ascertain for

yourself. I hope you see now how important it is to feed your cat with bread and milk. If you were to let it eat nothing but mice and birds it might grow larger and fiercer, and scalier and tailier, and get wings and become the beginning of dragons. Then of course there would be all this bother all over again.

The Two Frogs

A Japanese folk tale retold by Andrew Lang

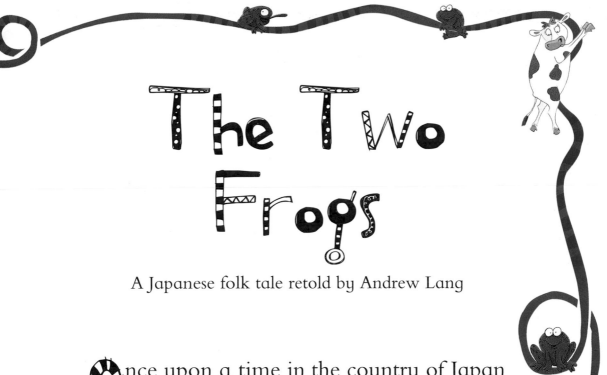

Once upon a time in the country of Japan there lived two frogs, one of whom made his home in a ditch near the town of Osaka, on the coast, while the other dwelt in a clear little stream that ran through the city of Kioto. At such a great distance apart, they had never heard of each other. But, funnily enough, the idea came into both their heads at once that they should like to see a little of the world.

The frog who lived at Kioto wanted to visit Osaka, and the frog who lived at Osaka wished to go to Kioto, where the great Mikado had his palace.

So one fine morning in the spring they both set out along the road that led from Kioto to Osaka, one from one end and the other from the other. The journey was more tiring than either had expected, for they did not know much about travelling, and halfway along the road there arose a mountain that had to be climbed. It took them both a long time and a great many hops to reach the top, but there they were at last.

Imagine how surprised each frog was to see another frog before him! They looked at each other for a moment without speaking, and then fell into conversation, discussing the cause of their meeting so far from their homes. They talked for a long time, and were delighted to find that they both had the same wish – to learn a little more of their native country.

As there was no sort of hurry, the two frogs stretched themselves out in a cool, damp place and agreed that they would have a good rest before they parted to go their separate ways.

"What a pity we are not bigger," said the Osaka frog, "for then we could see both towns from here, and tell if it is worth our while going on."

"Oh, that is easily managed," returned the Kioto frog. "We have only got to stand up on our hind legs, and hold on to each other, and then we can each look at the town we are travelling to."

This idea pleased the Osaka frog so much that he at once jumped up and put his front feet on the shoulders of his friend, who had risen onto his hind legs also. There they both stood, stretching themselves as high as they could and

The Two Frogs

holding each other tightly, so that they
would not fall down.

The Kioto frog turned his nose towards
Osaka, and the Osaka frog turned his nose
towards Kioto. But the foolish creatures
forgot that when they stood up their eyes
lay in the backs of their great heads. So
although their noses were pointing to the

places to which they wanted to go, their eyes were actually looking at the places from which they had come.

"Dear me!" cried the Osaka frog. "Kioto is exactly like Osaka. It is certainly not worth such a long journey. I shall go back home instead!"

"If I had had any idea that Osaka was only a copy of Kioto I should never have travelled all this way," exclaimed the frog from Kioto, and as he spoke he took his feet from his friend's shoulders, and they both fell down on the grass.

Both frogs were disappointed at their discoveries. They took a polite farewell of each other, and set off for home again. And to the end of their lives they believed

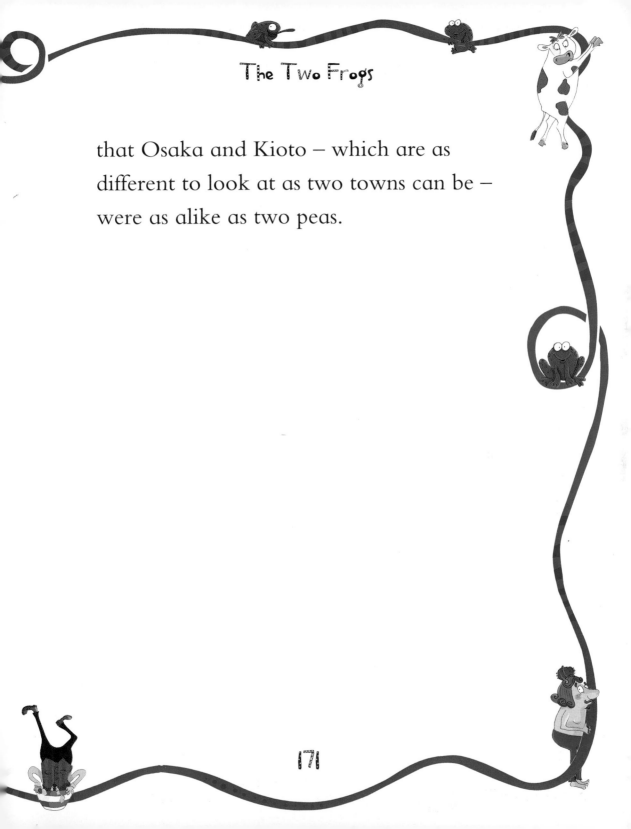

that Osaka and Kioto – which are as different to look at as two towns can be – were as alike as two peas.

The Milkmaid and her Pail

An Aesop's fable

A farmer's daughter had just completed her morning milking and was carrying a pail of milk from the field to the farmhouse, when it set her thinking. 'When this milk is sold,' she mused, 'the money it fetches will buy at least three hundred eggs. Even allowing for some of the eggs not to hatch, we should end up with at least two hundred and fifty chickens. If we feed and look after the chickens well, they will grow up to achieve the highest price at market.

'So, when they are all sold and Father gives me my share of the proceeds, I shall have enough money to buy a beautiful new gown – maybe even that pink one with rosebuds all over it in the seamstress's window in the village.

'How fabulous I will look in it! I will wear it to every party this Christmas. None of the lads from any of the villages round about will be able to keep their eyes off me. They will all want to talk to me, and dance with me, and even propose to me – but I will toss my head and refuse them, every one of them.'

And with that, she tossed her head vainly and turned on her heel, pretending to scorn a suitor's hand in marriage. But at the sudden movement, the heavy milk pail slipped from her hand. *Crash!* It fell to the ground and the milk spilled everywhere and ran

away – along with all her foolish imaginings…

Brer Rabbit and the Moon in the Pond

Adapted from an *Uncle Remus* story
by Joel Chandler Harris

Every now and again Brer Fox and Brer Rabbit would shake hands and make peace for a while and, following their example, all the critters would forget their arguments and get along together just fine and dandy. It had been like this for some weeks when Brer Rabbit ran into Brer

Turtle, and the two got talking.

"It sure is peaceful around here now," sighed Brer Rabbit.

"Yep," nodded Brer Turtle, who was a critter of few words.

"It sure is quiet," sighed Brer Rabbit.

"Yep," nodded Brer Turtle.

"Peaceful and quiet is good, but it ain't fun like in the old days, is it, Brer Turtle?" asked Brer Rabbit.

"Nope," agreed Brer Turtle.

"I think that the folks round here could do with a good dose of fun again," sighed Brer Rabbit.

"Yep," nodded Brer Turtle.

Brer Rabbit bounced to his feet with a chuckle. "Then I'm going to invite

everyone to a little fishing frolic at the pond
tomorrow night," he said. "I'll do all the
talking as long as you back me up with
your 'yep's and 'nope's now and then."

Brer Rabbit and Brer Turtle shook
hands in agreement. Brer Rabbit bounded
off to do the inviting and Brer Turtle set
out for the pond, so he'd be sure to get
there on time…

Sure enough, the following night
everyone was there at the pond, ready to
fish. Brer Bear and Brer Turtle had brought
their hooks and lines. Brer Wolf carried a
pot of wriggling bait. Brer Fox brought his
fishing net. Miss Meadows and Miss Motts
brought themselves, dressed up to the nines.

While Brer Wolf shook his pot at

Miss Meadows and Miss Motts and made them squeal with delight, Brer Bear announced he was going to fish for mud-cats. Brer Turtle said he was going to fish for horneyheads. Brer Fox declared he was going to fish for perch for the ladies. And Brer Rabbit winked at Brer Turtle and said he was going to fish for suckers.

So everyone got busy readying their hooks and their lines and their bait, and Brer Rabbit went to the edge of the pond to cast his line first. "I don't believe it!" he gasped, peering into the water and scratching his head. "The moon has gone and fell in the water!"

Everyone looked serious and gathered round and tut-tutted and well-welled and

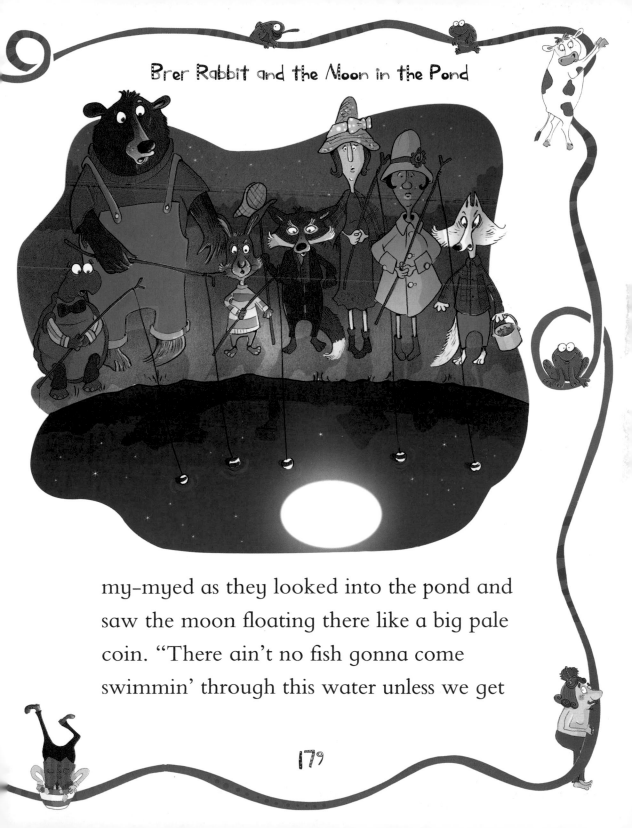

my-myed as they looked into the pond and saw the moon floating there like a big pale coin. "There ain't no fish gonna come swimmin' through this water unless we get

179

the moon out of the way," said Brer Rabbit. "Isn't that so, Brer Turtle?"

"Yep," nodded Brer Turtle, with a twinkle in his eye.

"So how we gonna get the moon out, Brer Rabbit?" worried Miss Meadows.

"Hmm," pondered Brer Rabbit. "I've got it! We borrow Brer Turtle's drag net, and we drag it across the pond, and we drag the moon right out!"

"That's it!" agreed everyone excitedly. "That's surely it!"

"It don't bother you none if we borrow your drag net, does it, Brer Turtle?" asked Brer Rabbit.

"Nope," replied Brer Turtle, trying hard not to collapse into laughter.

Then Brer Rabbit leapt off to fetch Brer
Turtle's drag net and was back again
before anyone could say 'lickety-spit'. "I
think I'd better be the one to do the
dragging," Brer Rabbit declared. "It needs
someone mighty clever and muscley."

At that, Brer Fox and Brer Bear and
Brer Wolf sprang forward and insisted on
taking the drag net from Brer Rabbit. After
all, they didn't want to look foolish in front
of the ladies, now did they?

Brer Fox and Brer Bear and Brer Wolf
walked gingerly to the edge of the pond
with the net. They cast it into the water,
dragged it along, and heaved it out,
dripping. When the ripples had settled on
the pond, there was the moon, shining just

as bright in the water as before.

"Nope!" cried Brer Rabbit. "You need to go into the pond."

Brer Fox and Brer Bear and Brer Wolf waded knee-deep into the cold pond. Once again they cast out the big drag net, and once again they pulled it in empty.

"Try again, a little deeper," yelled Brer Rabbit from the nice, dry bank. "You'll surely get it next time." Miss Meadows and Miss Motts eagerly waved them further out.

Brer Fox and Brer Bear and Brer Wolf took one more step… and suddenly the bottom of the pond fell away steeply and there was no more mud under their feet and they were ducked right under the water! Up they popped, choking and

splashing and spluttering.

Miss Meadows and Miss Motts and Brer Turtle and Brer Rabbit laughed and laughed, and then laughed some more as Brer Fox and Brer Bear and Brer Wolf hauled themselves out of the pond. They were a sight for sore eyes, dripping water from every bit of fur and covered all over in waterweed.

"I've heard that the moon will always bite if you use fools for bait," Brer Rabbit giggled, looking them up and down with satisfied glee. "Now if you're asking me, you gentlemen ought to hurry yourselves home and get into some dry clothes."

Brer Fox and Brer Bear and Brer Wolf had to grudgingly admit that Brer Rabbit had got the better of them. They slopped and slapped and squelched away into the moonlight.

The Bearded Fool

An Indian fable

Once upon a time there lived a man with a very long beard that reached down past his waist. He was very proud of his beard and washed and combed it every day. 'My long beard makes me look so intelligent, like a professor,' he would think, admiring himself in the mirror.

One evening, the man sat up late, reading by candlelight. He was really enjoying his book – a popular tome of proverbs and wise sayings – until he came to a sentence that read: "Any man with a long beard is a fool."

'What?' he thought. 'That can't be right – I can't have read that correctly!' And he read the sentence again, very carefully: "Any man with a long beard is a fool."

The man was most dismayed. "But I always thought my long beard made me look so scholarly!" he cried. "I have been wrong all along. And all this time, everyone has been thinking I am a fool!"

The man felt so disappointed and embarrassed that he decided to get rid of his long beard at once. He hunted high and low for a pair of scissors. He knew he had some somewhere, but could he find them –

no. And of course, he hadn't had a razor in the house for a very long time.

Immensely frustrated, the man grabbed the offending hair in his hands and without thinking, thrust the tip over the flame of a candle. It caught fire at once – but the flames licked up the length of his beard much faster than he had expected. In just a moment, the hair was all gone and the fire was singeing his chin. Next, his moustache caught fire. Then a spark leapt up into the hair on his head and that started burning too. "Aaaaiiiiieeeee!" the man screeched. How it hurt! Within moments, the hair on his head was all burnt to ash.

The man's screams of panic brought his neighbours running at once. How shocked they were to see his scorched face and head, surrounded by little wisps of smoke.

"What on earth happened to you?" they cried, splashing him with water.

"It was destiny," said the man, sadly. "I read that men with long beards were fools, and indeed, I have proved it!"

189

The Husband Who Was to Mind the House

Adapted from a Norse folk tale told
by Sir George Webbe Dasent

Once upon a time there was a man who was always surly and cross. He never thought his wife did anything right in the house. So one evening, his wife said: "Dear love, don't be so angry – there's a good man. Tomorrow let's swap our work. I'll go out with the harvesters, and you stay here and mind the house."

The husband thought that would do very well.

So, early next morning, his wife took a scythe and went out into the hayfield, leaving the man to do the housework.

First, the man set to churning the butter. It was thirsty work, and after a while he went down to the cellar to tap a barrel of ale. But, just when he had knocked in the bung and was putting the tap into the cask, he heard the pig come into the kitchen overhead. Off he ran up the cellar steps with the tap in his hand, as fast as he could.

But by the
time he got
there, the pig had
already knocked over the churn. It stood
there, grunting, among the cream – which
was running all over the floor.

The man was wild with rage. Then all

at once he remembered he still had the tap in his hand! By the time he got back down to the cellar, every drop of ale had run out of the cask. Furious, he began to churn what cream was left, for they needed butter for dinner. However, when he had churned a bit, he remembered that their milking cow was still shut up in the barn, and hadn't had a bite to eat or a drop to drink all the morning.

'It's too far to take her down to the meadow,' he thought. 'I'll just take her up to the roof to graze,' – for the house was roofed with turf and a fine crop of grass was growing there.

Now their house stood close against a steep hill, and he thought if he laid a plank across to the roof he'd easily get the cow up. But he couldn't leave the churn in the kitchen, for his little baby was crawling around on the floor and he feared she might tip it over. So he strapped the churn onto his back and went out with it. First, he stopped at the well to draw water for the cow to drink before he turned her out on the roof. But as he stooped over, all the cream ran out of the churn, over his shoulders, and disappeared down into the well.

It was now nearing dinner-time, so he thought he'd best hurry up and boil the porridge. Once he'd turned out the cow, he filled the pot with water and set it over the fire. When he had done that, he began to

worry that the cow might perhaps fall off
the roof. So he got up there to tie her up.
He fastened one end of the rope to the
cow's collar, and the other he threw down
the chimney. Then he went back inside and
fastened the loose end around his own leg.

Hurriedly, he began to grind the
oatmeal… but while he was at it, down fell
the cow off the roof after all! As she fell, she
dragged the man up the chimney by the
rope, feet first. There he remained, stuck
fast. As for the cow, she hung halfway
down the wall, swinging between heaven
and earth, for she could get neither down
nor up.

Now when the wife got home and saw
the cow hanging in such a manner, she ran

straight up to the roof and cut the rope in two with her scythe.

Of course, as she did this, down came her husband out of the chimney… so when the wife entered the kitchen, she found him standing on his head in the porridge-pot.

The Celebrated Jumping Frog of Calaveras County

Adapted from the story by Mark Twain

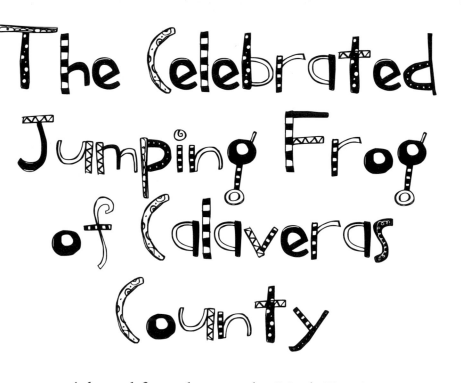

An old friend wrote to me and told me to be sure I made the acquaintance of a neighbour, Simon Wheeler, to ask after my friend's childhood companion, Leonidas W Smiley. So I did – and here's what happened. I have to say that I now suspect there is no such person as Leonidas W Smiley, that my friend made him up to get old Simon Wheeler to tell me his long, exasperating story about another man called Smiley. If my friend's aim was to fool me into sitting with a man who talks your ears off, then I fell right for it.

I found Simon Wheeler in the tavern, dozing by the fire. He roused at my approach and said good-day. I told him a friend had asked me to inquire about a Leonidas W Smiley.

Immediately, old Simon Wheeler backed me into a corner and trapped me there with his chair. "Well, I can't say I know any Leonidas W Smiley," he began, "but there was a feller here by the name of Jim Smiley in the winter of '49 – or maybe the spring of '50 – I don't recollect exactly, though what makes me think it were one or the other is the big chimney weren't built in the mining camp when he came…

"Anyways, he was a gambler through and through – the sorta man who'd bet on anythin', long as he could find someone to bet against him, and if he couldn't, he'd change sides and bet the other way himself. If there was two birds on a fence, he'd bet you which would fly first. If he saw a long-legged straddle-bug beetle start to go somewhere, he'd bet you how long it would take him to get wherever he was going. And if you took him up on the bet, he would follow that straddle-bug anywheres till he found out where he was going and how long it took – all the way to Mexico, if he had to.

"Lots of the boys here knew Smiley and can tell you 'bout him. He'd bet on anythin'. And Smiley was lucky with it – uncommonly lucky – he always came out on top…

"Well, 'cept for the time Smiley caught a frog. He said he calculated to educate him. He did nothing for three months 'cept sit in his backyard and teach that frog to jump. And you bet he did teach him, too. He'd give him a little nudge behind and next minute you'd see that frog whirling through the air like a doughnut. You'd see him turn

one somersault, or maybe a couple, if he
got a good start. And he'd always land on
his feet, like a cat. Smiley got him
practising catching flies too, until that frog
only needed to look at a fly and it was his.

"Smiley said all a frog needed was
education and he could do almost anythin'
– and I believe him. Why, I've seen him set
Dan'l Webster down here on this floor –
Dan'l Webster was the frog's name – and
sing out, 'Flies, Dan'l, flies!' and quicker
than you could wink he'd spring straight up
and snake a fly off the counter there. Then
he'd flop down again, solid as a gob of
mud, and scratch the side of his head with
his hind foot as if he'd done no more than
any other frog might do.

"You never saw a frog so modest and straightforward as him, for all he was so gifted. And when it came to fair and square jumping on level ground, he could jump further than any other frog in God's creation. Long-jumping on level ground was that frog's speciality, you understand. Smiley was monstrous proud of his frog, and well he might be, for fellers that had travelled and been everywheres all said he was the most amazin' frog they ever saw.

"Now Smiley kept Dan'l Webster in a little box and every now and again he'd bring him out for a bet. One day a feller – a stranger in town – comes across him and says: 'What might it be that you've got in that box?'

"And Smiley says, sorta indifferent-like, 'It's just a frog.'

"And the feller took it, and turned it this way and that, and said, 'Hmm, so 'tis. What's he good for?'

"'Well,' Smiley says, 'he can outjump any frog in Calaveras County.'

"The feller took the box again, took a long look, and then gave it back. 'Well,' he says, 'I don't see nothin' about that frog that's any better than any other frog.'

"'Maybe you don't,' Smiley says. 'Anyways, I'll risk forty dollars that he can outjump any frog in Calaveras County.'

"And the feller thought a minute, and then said, 'Well, I ain't got no frog, but if I had a frog, I'd bet you.'

"Then Smiley says, 'That's alright. If you'll hold my box, I'll go and get you a frog.' And so Smiley went off and the feller waited. He sat there a good while, thinking to himself. Then suddenly he got out a little bag from his pocket – filled with lead shot it was, the smallest kind, the sort you use for hunting quails. He got the frog out of the box, opened his mouth and took a teaspoon and filled him full of lead shot – filled, I tell you! Then he put him down on the ground.

"Meanwhile, Smiley came back with a frog he caught in the swamp. He gives the new frog to this feller and says: 'Now if you're ready, set him right alongside Dan'l, with his forepaws even with Dan'l's, and I'll give the word.' Then he calls out,

'One… two… three… get!' And him and
the feller touched the frogs from behind.

"The new frog hopped off lively. But
though Dan'l give a heave, he couldn't
budge – he was planted as solid as a
church! Smiley was a good deal surprised,

and he was disgusted too, but he didn't have no idea what the matter was, of course, not a clue. So the feller took Smiley's money, and as he was leaving, he commented casually, 'I still don't see nothin' about that frog that's any better than any other frog.'"

Here Simon Wheeler heard his name called from the tavern's front yard and stood up to see what was wanted. It was nothing important, and so he sat straight back down and began again. "Where was I?" he continued with a grin. "Oh yes, well, this here Smiley also had a yellow, one-eyed cow that didn't have no tail, only just a short stump like a little banana you see, and so Smiley—"

At that, I stood and bid the old gentleman good-day, and politely took my leave.

Trickster Tales

last chance to let me go!" Brer Rabbit hollered. "I mean it! If you don't release me, I'll make you pay, good and proper."

But the tar baby didn't utter a sound and didn't move a muscle.

"No? Really! Right, you've had it now!" Brer Rabbit screamed. *THUNK!* He head-butted the tar baby and found himself stuck eye-to-eye with the cheeky critter.

All this time, Brer Fox had been holding in so much laughter he thought he was going to burst. Now he leapt out of his hiding place and cried, "My oh my, Brer Rabbit! What kind of mess have you got yourself into this time?"

"I suppose you're gonna have yourself a tasty barbecued bunny for supper this evening," Brer Rabbit admitted.

"Yep! You said it," grinned Brer Fox, licking his lips.

"Well, I'm glad you're going to dress me up with some sauce and warm me over your fire," Brer Rabbit smiled. "I'd much rather you did that than throw me in that briar patch over there."

'Hang on a minute,' thought Brer Fox, his face falling, 'that no-good rabbit seems quite pleased about being roasted!'

"I've changed my mind," Brer Fox said out loud. "I'm gonna hang you instead."

"Ain't I glad it's a good old hangin' and not being thrown in the briar patch!" sighed Brer Rabbit.

Brer Fox frowned. "I mean, I'm gonna

drown you!" he declared.

"Fine, fine…" replied Brer Rabbit lightly. "Dip me in the water and at least I'll die clean. Just don't throw me in that there briar patch, that's all!"

Brer Fox was then sure that the very worst thing he could do to Brer Rabbit was to hurl him into the prickly briar patch. He grabbed him round the waist and pulled him hard, and – *shlup!* – Brer Rabbit came unstuck from the tar baby. Holding him tightly, Brer Fox spun round and round and round and – *wheeeee!* – Brer Rabbit went sailing high into the air and came down – *thump!* – in the briar patch.

Brer Fox's face broke into a

broad grin. "I've bested that bunny once and for all!" he chuckled, wiping his hands.

But a high-pitched giggle came from the far side of the briar patch. When Brer Fox squinted into the sunshine, he could just see Brer Rabbit hopping away into the distance. "I was born and bred in a briar patch, Brer Fox!" he was singing gleefully. "Hee hee! Born and bred in a briar patch!"

Filled with rage, Brer Fox thumped the very first thing that came to hand. And you know what that was, don't you?

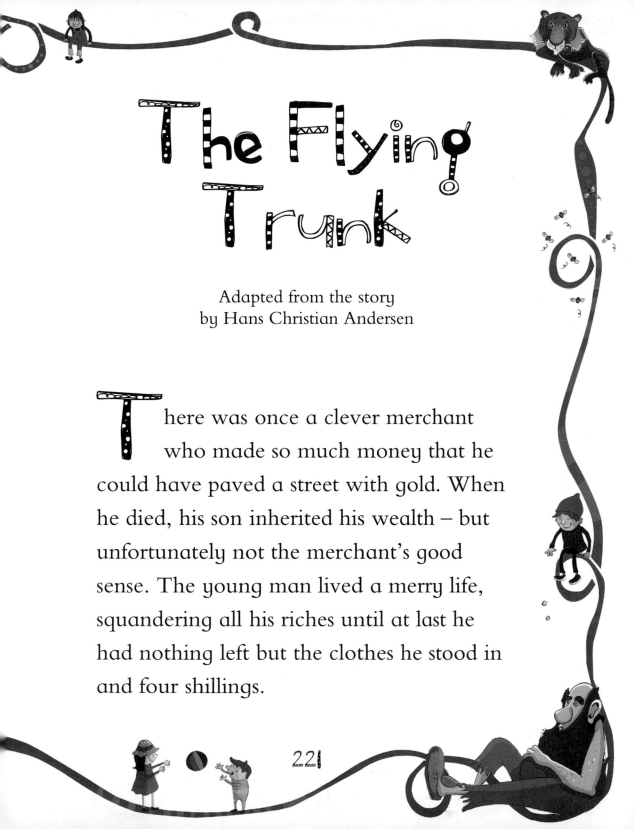

The Flying Trunk

Adapted from the story
by Hans Christian Andersen

There was once a clever merchant who made so much money that he could have paved a street with gold. When he died, his son inherited his wealth – but unfortunately not the merchant's good sense. The young man lived a merry life, squandering all his riches until at last he had nothing left but the clothes he stood in and four shillings.

TRICKSTER TALES

Of course, all his so-called friends deserted him. One of them even mocked him by sending him an old trunk with the message: "Pack up and get lost!"

"I would," the young man sighed, "if I had anything left to pack up. Maybe I should just pack myself up…" He climbed into the trunk and sat there, fiddling with the lock.

To his great amazement, as he pressed on it he felt a sudden jolt upwards. For the trunk was magic and flew away when anyone pressed the lock. Now it rocketed up the chimney and into the sky. It soared through the clouds, all the way to Turkey, where it gently came to rest in the middle of a wood.

The Flying Trunk

When the trunk was no longer moving, the young man clambered out. Tingling with excitement, he hid the trunk under some dry leaves and made his way to a nearby city. The streets were bustling with people. The young man spotted a mighty palace rising above the other buildings. He introduced himself to a passer-by and asked who lived there.

"Why, the sultan's daughter lives there," the woman replied. "It has been foretold that she will fall in love with a trickster, and therefore no one is allowed to visit her unless the king and queen are present."

"Thank you," said the merchant's son. He thought for a while, then hurried back to the wood, seated himself in the trunk and flew up to the roof of the palace. He crept through a window into the princess's room, where she lay sleeping.

As he stood watching her, she woke up and was very frightened. The young man told a fib – he said he was an angel who had come down from heaven to see her. This pleased the princess very much.

So the young man sat by her side and talked to her. He told her that her eyes were like beautiful dark lakes, in which thoughts swam about like little mermaids, and that her skin was like a soft plain. When he asked her if she would marry him, she agreed straight away.

"Come on Saturday," she said, "for my parents will be here for tea. How proud they will be when they find out I am going to marry an angel! But to win them over, you must think of a wonderful story to tell them, for they like stories better than anything."

"Very well," he replied, "I will bring them the gift of my very best tale." And so they parted.

When the 'angel' returned on Saturday, the king and queen received him with great politeness and curiosity.

"As you are an angel, you must have a wonderful story for us," remarked the king.

"Oh yes," said the queen, "please do tell us a tale."

"Certainly," the young man replied. "There was once a merchant's son," he began, "who had fallen on hard times. But luck soon came his way – he discovered a magical flying trunk. He soared away to a far-off country, where he met a beautiful princess. To gain her trust, he told her he was an angel.

"The princess was under a cruel enchantment that had taken away her wits and turned her into a fool – and not just her, but also her father and mother, the king and queen. However, the young man had heard many fairy stories on his travels and knew just how to break the spell –

obviously, he had to kiss the princess! The moment he had done so, the curse was lifted – the royal family were fools no more and could see everything clearly again.

"The princess married the merchant's son and of course, they all lived happily ever after," the young man finished, his fingers crossed hopefully behind his back.

"What an exciting story!" cried the king. "I really feel as if it had happened to me!"

"Yes, you certainly are a storyteller like no other!" agreed the queen. "You must marry our daughter and join our family! I can hardly wait for all the tales with which you are going to entertain us."

Only the princess sat still and silent, deep in thought.

The wedding day was fixed, and the evening before, a great festival was held in the city so everyone could celebrate. Coloured lanterns were lit, cakes and sweets were thrown among the people, and bands played music so everyone could dance in the streets. Altogether, it was a splendid affair.

'I will give everyone a treat of my own,' thought the merchant's son. So he took the four shillings, which was all the money he had left in the world, and went and bought

The Flying Trunk

all sorts of fireworks. He packed them in his trunk and flew up into the air.

What a tremendous show they made as they went off! And how amazed everyone

229

was to see him flying around in the sky! The people really believed him to be an angel.

But alas, a spark from one of the fireworks landed on the flying trunk and set it alight. The merchant's son only just made it back down to the ground safely before the smouldering object burst into flames and burned away to ashes.

So the merchant's son could not fly any more, nor go to meet his bride. But perhaps that was just as well. The princess had realized that she had been tricked and was waiting to kick him out of the kingdom, for of course she didn't want to marry a liar – flying trunk or no flying trunk.

Today, the foolish merchant's son

wanders through the world making a living by telling fairytales – but none of them are as entertaining as his own story.

That's Not True!

A Hungarian fairytale retold by Baroness Orczy

Once upon a time there was a princess who was very beautiful – and also determinedly single. She did not want to marry any old prince or nobleman, so she thought up what she was sure was an impossible challenge for would-be suitors. The princess announced publicly that she would only marry the man who could tell her father, the king, a story that he could not believe.

That's Not True!

Of course, the whole point of being a gallant prince or a bold knight is that you are not put off by a challenge. So, to the princess's great dismay, noble suitors streamed to the castle from hundreds of miles around.

And what incredible stories they told! Many had travelled on brave quests across wide seas, through deep dark forests, over scorching deserts, up icy mountains that scraped the sky, and far into the depths of underground caverns. They told fantastic stories of the dragons and monsters they had fought, the witches and warlocks they had outwitted, the demons, dwarves and goblins they had tricked, and the curses and enchantments they had overcome.

But the king was old and had heard it all before. After all, he had been a young prince once and had gone out into the world to seek adventures and make his name. He had faced much magic, many perils and pestilences. Nothing was new to him. Nothing was unbelievable.

So the flood of noble suitors gradually dwindled to a stream, thinned to a trickle, and then dried up altogether.

Now in a nearby village there dwelt a poor young peasant called John, who had heard about the princess's announcement. One day, he summoned all his courage and strode up to the king's castle. Although he was trembling on the inside, he knocked firmly at the gates and demanded an audience with His Majesty.

The king knew very well what the young fellow wanted. Even though John wasn't noble, so many princes and knights had come on the same errand and failed that the king was despairing that his daughter would ever marry. And what the king wanted most to cheer him in his old age was to hear the laughter of his grandchildren around the castle, and have them curl up on his lap as he sat on his throne, telling them his incredible stories. So the king gave the order for the young peasant to be admitted to the royal presence at once.

"Good morning, Your Majesty," John said, a little nervously.

"Good morning, my lad. Well, what do you want?" asked the king kindly.

"Please, Your Majesty, I have come as a suitor for your daughter."

"Very good," encouraged the king. "But I'm sorry to have to say it – you don't look as though you have a penny to your name. May I ask in what manner you would be able to keep her?"

"I dare say I could manage to keep her pretty comfortably indeed. My father owns a pig."

"Really?" said the king.

"A wonderful pig, Your Majesty," the lad went on. "This pig has kept my father, my mother, seven sisters, and myself, for the last twenty years."

"Indeed!" said the king, wondering how this was possible.

"He gives us as good a quart of milk every morning as any cow," said John.

237

"Indeed!" said the king, stroking his beard. "I suspect this is a magical pig then," he remarked.

"Yes sire, and he lays most delicious eggs for our breakfast," John remarked.

"Indeed!" said the king, scratching his head. "It must be a very strong magic," he said thoughtfully.

"And every day my mother cuts a nice bit of bacon out of his side, and every night it grows back again," John insisted.

"Indeed!" said the king, his eyes widening. "As I thought, an exceedingly strong and powerful magic."

"The other day the pig disappeared. My mother looked for him high and low, all over the village, but he was nowhere to be seen," continued John.

"That must have been very sad," replied the king.

"Oh, it was, sire," agreed John. "But there was a happy ending. She finally found him in the larder, catching mice."

"Intelligent too – what a useful pig!" said the king, chuckling.

"He is exceedingly useful – my father sends him into town every day to do errands for him," John went on.

"How wise of your father," remarked the king.

"He ordered all of my father's clothes, and indeed mine too, from Your Majesty's own tailor."

"They do appear very well made!" said

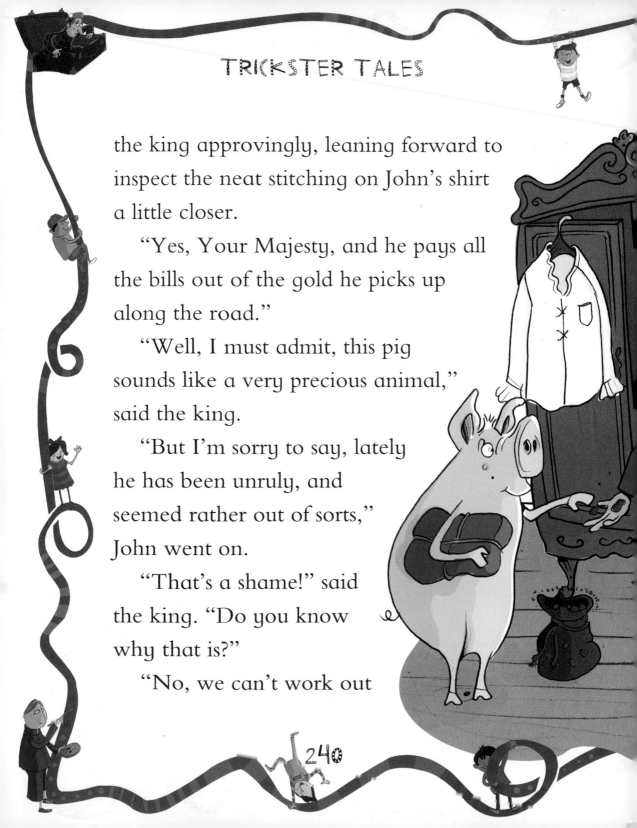

the king approvingly, leaning forward to inspect the neat stitching on John's shirt a little closer.

"Yes, Your Majesty, and he pays all the bills out of the gold he picks up along the road."

"Well, I must admit, this pig sounds like a very precious animal," said the king.

"But I'm sorry to say, lately he has been unruly, and seemed rather out of sorts," John went on.

"That's a shame!" said the king. "Do you know why that is?"

"No, we can't work out

the reason," sighed John. "He refuses to go where he is told, and won't allow my mother to have any more bacon from his side."

"Have you tried punishing him?" inquired the king, most intrigued.

"We can't bring ourselves to do that, Your Majesty," explained John. "We are so fond of the pig after all he has done for us, and we feel so sorry for him, as he is growing rather blind and can no longer see where he is going."

"What a shame! Yes, yes, you're right, of course. He should really be treated with the utmost kindness," agreed the king.

241

"Yes, Your Majesty, that is why my father has just engaged your father to be our pig-keeper," stated John.

"That's not true!" yelled the king, outraged at the peasant's unbelievably bold claim. Then suddenly he remembered his daughter's challenge…

So the king ordered the princess to marry the peasant. He never regretted it – and neither did she. For John was a most clever and amiable young man, and the princess soon fell deeply in love with him.

The couple lived happily in the castle with the king for very many years. They had several little sons and daughters who loved nothing better than to sit on the king's lap in his big throne while he told

them his incredible stories. And years later,
when John became king himself, all his
people declared they had never had so wise
and witty a ruler.

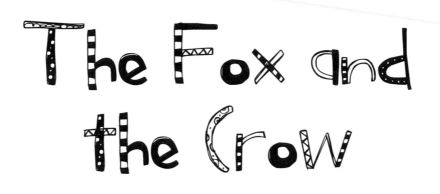

The Fox and the Crow

Retold from an Aesop's fable

Once upon a time there lived a big black crow in a forest. One day she was perched on a branch, preening her sleek, glossy feathers and admiring herself in the stream below, when she spied a piece of cheese on the bank. She swooped down and picked up the tasty morsel in her beak. Then she flew back to the tree where she settled once more on a branch, the cheese held tightly in her beak so all her neighbours could see how clever and lucky she was.

Unbeknown to the crow, a wily fox was lurking in some bushes below. He saw what the crow had done and licked his lips at the thought of the delicious cheese. But how could he get it for himself? He needed to come up with a plan fast, before the crow grew tired of showing off the delicacy and ate it up.

Then all at once the fox had an idea. He strolled casually to the foot of the tree.

"Mistress Crow," he cried out, "how lovely you look today! How gleaming your feathers are, how sharp your beak and how wonderfully bright your eyes! I'm sure your voice must be just as beautiful. Do let me hear it – please sing for me. Then I will go and tell everyone that you truly are the Queen of Birds."

Of course, the vain crow was thrilled by these words, and was more than happy to oblige. Without thinking, she lifted her head, tilted her beak proudly to the skies, and began to caw her coarse song. The cheese tumbled to the ground.

The gleeful fox pounced on it at once, snapping it up in his jaws. "Thank you, that was all I wanted," he said, swallowing the last morsel with a grin. "And in exchange for your most delicious cheese I will give you a piece of advice you would do well to remember in future – when people pay you compliments, they may not

The Fox and the Crow

always be telling the truth."

And the moral of the story is: do not trust flatterers.

Stan Bolovan

An Eastern European folk tale
told by Andrew Lang

A long time ago, a small, ramshackle
house stood all alone on a moor. In
the house lived a poor man named Stan
Bolovan and his wife and their children –
so many children that the couple had lost
count of how many they had. Certainly too
many for a poor man to feed.

There came a time when the family had
eaten all the food in the house and there

was no money to buy more. Stan decided he must go out into the world to find some.

So Stan wandered and wandered and wandered till he reached the end of the world, and there he saw a shepherd with an enormous flock of sheep.

Stan waited till midnight and then crept up to the sheep, hoping he might steal some. But he was stopped in his tracks by a rushing noise, and through the air flew a big dragon, who swooped down and grabbed several sheep in his talons, before soaring off again. After this, Stan was too terrified to move.

The same thing happened the next night – and the next. And each morning, the shepherd moaned and groaned that he

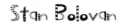

could do nothing about it.

Stan thought of his hungry children at home and at last made himself known to the shepherd and said, "What will you give me if I rid you of the dragon?"

"Half of my flock, most willingly," answered the shepherd.

Stan thought of the fearsome dragon, but then he considered how long all those sheep would feed his starving children. "It's a deal," he replied firmly.

Just before midnight Stan positioned himself in the centre of the flock. Once again there was the sudden rush of air and the dragon came swooping down.

"Dear me!" exclaimed the dragon. "Who are you, small man, and where did you come from?"

"I am Stan Bolovan," roared Stan at
the top of his voice, although he was
quaking inside. "I eat rocks all night and
in the day I feed on the flowers of the
mountain. These sheep are *mine!* And if
you meddle with them once more I will
carve you up into tiny pieces."

When the dragon heard these words he quailed, for no one had ever spoken to him like that before. He presumed that this Stan Bolovan must be a mighty hero, just like the ones he had heard about in all the old stories.

The fearful dragon thought quickly and came up with a plan to lure Stan home to where his mother was waiting, for she was bigger and much stronger than he. "Now don't be hasty," said the quaking dragon. "If you promise not to carve me into tiny pieces I will pay you seven sacks of gold coins. Come home with me now and I'll give them to you."

Seven sacks full of gold coins! Stan agreed at once,

and started along the road with the dragon.

The dragon's mother was as old as time itself. When she saw that her son had come home without any sheep she grew very angry and flames darted from her nostrils. But before she could speak, the dragon whispered in her ear: "Mother, this man eats rocks all night and in the day feasts on the flowers of the mountain. He carves dragons into tiny pieces! He's a proper hero, like in the old days."

"There is no need to be afraid," muttered the wise, old dragon in reply. "You did the right thing in bringing him here to me. We'll just wait until he is asleep. Then you take your club and hit him on the head. It is easily done."

And so it would have been if Stan hadn't outwitted them. That night, when the dragon and his mother had put out their lights, he stuffed an old sack with earth. Then he placed it in his bed and covered it with clothes, while he hid himself under the bed – just in case. He then began to snore very loudly.

Very soon the dragon came creeping into the room, and landed a tremendous blow on the spot where Stan's head should have been. Stan groaned loudly from under the bed, and, satisfied, the dragon stole away as softly as he had come.

Next morning, the dragon and his mother were having a slap-up breakfast when Stan came strolling down the stairs.

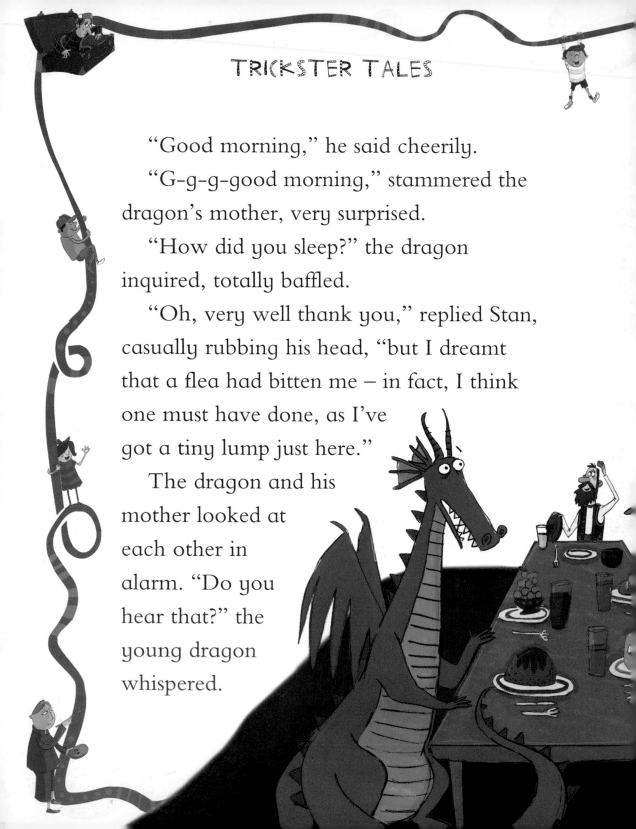

"Good morning," he said cheerily.

"G-g-g-good morning," stammered the dragon's mother, very surprised.

"How did you sleep?" the dragon inquired, totally baffled.

"Oh, very well thank you," replied Stan, casually rubbing his head, "but I dreamt that a flea had bitten me — in fact, I think one must have done, as I've got a tiny lump just here."

The dragon and his mother looked at each other in alarm. "Do you hear that?" the young dragon whispered.

"He thinks it was a flea – I broke my club on his head!"

This time the mother grew as frightened as her son. It appeared that nothing could be done to defeat a man like this, so she made all haste to fill seven sacks with gold coins, to get rid of Stan as soon as possible.

Stan stood still as they rushed about, trying not to let them see him trembling. What would the dragons do when they saw he could not lift even one sack?

When the seven sacks were full to bursting with gold, Stan looked at them without moving.

"What are you waiting for?" asked the dragon.

"Well, do you know, I think I quite like it here," Stan sighed. "Do you mind if I stay a little longer?"

The mother dragon's face fell and her son gave a little shriek of dismay. "I'll tell you what," the mother dragon said, "let's make it eight sacks – and my son will carry them home for you himself." The words were hardly out of her mouth before the young dragon had snatched up the eight sacks of gold and piled them on his back. Then he and Stan set off.

They travelled and travelled, and at length Stan caught sight of his ramshackle

house and heard his children's voices. The
boys and girls had had nothing to eat since
Stan left, and they were starving. They
came rushing towards him waving knives

and forks in their hands. At the sight of the dragon, they began to call out, "We will eat dragon's flesh, give us dragon's flesh!"

The dragon flung down the sacks in terror and flew away as fast as he could, back to the end of the world. And from that day to this, the dragons have never dared to show their faces again.

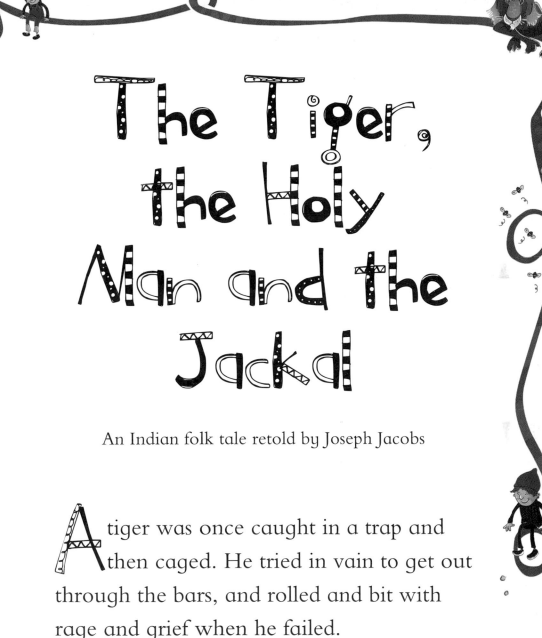

The Tiger, the Holy Man and the Jackal

An Indian folk tale retold by Joseph Jacobs

A tiger was once caught in a trap and then caged. He tried in vain to get out through the bars, and rolled and bit with rage and grief when he failed.

By chance a poor holy man came

walking by. "Have mercy on me and let me out of this cage, please, oh holy one!" cried the tiger.

"Nay, my friend," replied the holy man mildly, "for you would probably eat me if I did."

"Not at all!" swore the tiger with many oaths. "On the contrary, I should be forever grateful and serve you as a slave!"

As the tiger sobbed and sighed and wept in distress, the holy man's heart softened, and at last he consented to open the door of the cage. Out popped the tiger, and seizing the poor man, he cried out: "What a fool you are!

What is going to stop me from eating you now? For after being cooped up so long I am terribly hungry!"

The holy man begged and pleaded for his life, so the tiger summoned the few scraps of good nature he had, and decided instead to leave the matter in the hands of the universe. He told the holy man to ask three things whether they thought the tiger should eat him or not – and he promised to abide by their decision.

So the trembling holy man first asked a pipal tree what it thought of the matter. But the pipal tree replied coldly,

263

"What have you got to complain about? Think about me – I give shade and shelter to everyone who passes by, but do they show me gratitude? No, they do not! In return for my kindness they tear down my branches to feed their cattle. So don't ask me for sympathy – I have none for you!"

With great dismay in his heart, the holy man then walked through the countryside a little way till he came across a buffalo turning a well-wheel. But he fared the same with the buffalo, for it answered in a booming voice, "You are a fool to expect gratitude. Look at me! While I gave the people milk they fed me on cotton-seed and oil-cake, but now I am no longer good for milking they make me work all day in the

blazing sun, and give me nothing but
rotting leftovers as fodder!"

The holy man then desperately asked the
road to give him its opinion. "My dear sir,"
said the road, "how foolish you are to
expect anything but greed! Here I am,
useful to all, yet everyone – rich and poor,
great and small – tramples on me as they
travel along, throwing their rubbish at me
as they go!"

At this, the holy man sorrowfully turned
to make his way back to the tiger, as he
had promised. On the way he met a jackal,
who called out, "What's the matter, holy
man? You look as miserable as a fish out
of water!"

The holy man told him all that had

265

occurred. "How very confusing!" said the jackal, when the holy man had finished. "Would you mind telling me over again, for everything has got so mixed up!"

So the holy man told his tale all over again, but the jackal shook his head in a distracted sort of way.

"It's very odd," he said, "but I still don't understand! It all seems to go in one ear and out the other. If you take me to the place where it all happened then perhaps I shall be able to give a judgement."

So they returned to the cage where the tiger was waiting for the holy man, sharpening his teeth and claws.

"You've been away a long time!" growled the savage beast. "But now that you have discovered how things really are in the world, let us begin our dinner."

'Our dinner!' thought the wretched holy man with a shudder of fear. 'What a remarkably delicate way of putting it!'

"Just give me five minutes, my lord," he pleaded, "in order that I may explain matters to the jackal here, who appears to be somewhat slow-witted."

The tiger consented and the holy man began the whole story over again, not missing a single detail and spinning as long a yarn as possible.

"Oh, my poor brain! Oh, my poor brain!" cried the jackal, wringing his paws in distress. "Let me see! How did it all begin? You were in the cage, and the tiger came walking by—"

"Rot!" interrupted the tiger. "What a fool you are! *I* was in the cage."

"Of course!" cried the jackal, trembling with fright. "Yes! I was in the cage – no I wasn't. Dear, dear! Where are my wits? Let me see… the tiger was in the holy man, and the cage came walking by – no, that's not it, either! Well, don't mind me, but begin your dinner, for I shall never understand!"

"Yes, you shall!" returned the tiger, in a rage of frustration at the jackal's stupidity. "I'll make you understand! Look here – I am the tiger…"

"Yes, my lord!"

"And that is the holy man…"

"Yes, my lord!"

"And that is the cage…"

"Yes, my lord!"

"And I was in the cage – do you understand now?"

"Yes – no – please, my lord…"

"Well?" cried the tiger impatiently.

"Please, my lord, how did you get in?"

"How? In the usual way, of course!"

"Oh, dear me! My head is beginning to whirl again! Please don't be angry, my lord, but what is 'the usual way'?"

At this the tiger lost patience and, jumping into the cage, cried, "This way! Now do you understand how it was?"

"Perfectly!" grinned the jackal, as he swiftly slammed the door, revealing at once

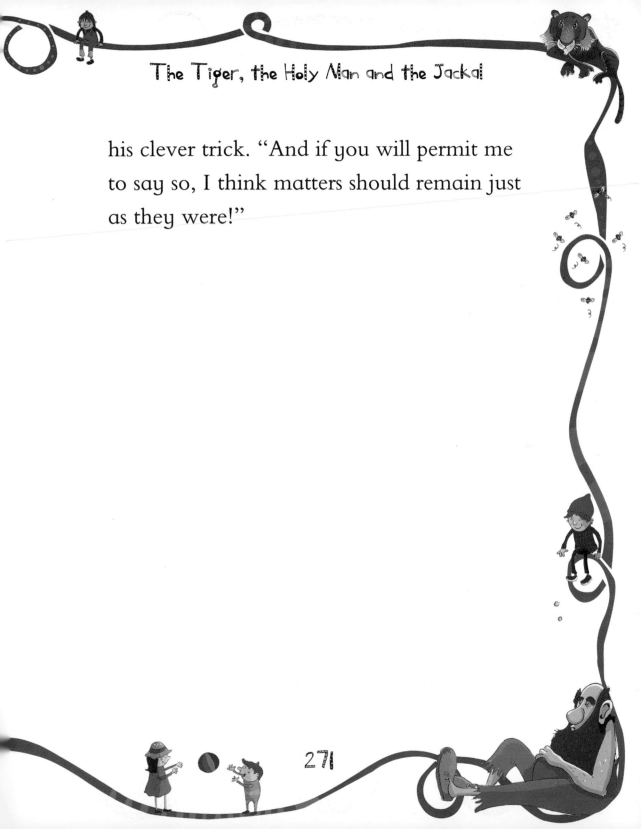

his clever trick. "And if you will permit me to say so, I think matters should remain just as they were!"

Thor's Journey to the Land of the Giants

Adapted from a Norse myth told
by Charles John Tibbit

One day, Thor the thunder god set out
from Asgard, home of the gods, in his
great rumbling chariot drawn by two goats.
He took with him the god of mischief,

Loki, for company, and one servant – a human boy named Thjalfi.

They travelled far to the east, eventually entering Jotunheim, the land of the giants. There they journeyed all day through an immense forest until, finally emerging from the trees, they saw a city situated in the middle of a vast plain. They approached it in wonder.

The city wall was so lofty that you could not see the top of it without throwing your head back. When they reached the wall, they found the gateway closed with immense bars across it, which even Thor could not have broken apart. So he and his companions crept between them.

The travellers found themselves standing

before a colossal palace. The door was
open, so they went in. They found
themselves in an enormous hall, filled with
hundreds of giant warriors. The giant in the
centre was clearly the king, Utgard-Loki,
whom they saluted with great respect.
However, he glanced at them and burst out

laughing. "If I'm not much mistaken," he boomed, "that little man there is the mighty thunder god, Thor!" And how all the giants laughed!

"I will give you a chance to prove that you are greater than your size," the giant king continued, to a roar of approval from his subjects. "Show us the best that you and your companions can do, and if you impress us, we promise we won't crush you – not today, at any rate."

Loki stepped forward without hesitation. "I can eat quicker than anyone else," he said, feeling confident (he was extremely hungry). "If there's anyone willing to compete with me, I will prove it."

So the king ordered one of his subjects,

Logi, to come forward, and try his skill against Loki. A great trough full of meat was placed in the hall. Loki positioned himself at one end and Logi set himself at the other. The two began to eat, gobbling through the meat and making quite a mess!

Presently they met in the middle of the trough, but Loki had only devoured the flesh of his portion, whereas the other had devoured both flesh and bones. All the company therefore decided that Loki had been beaten.

Then the boy Thjalfi declared that no man alive could beat him at running. So the king called forward a young giant named Hugi. "Ready… go!" he bellowed, and the two runners sped away. However,

Hugi ran so fast that he flashed around the enormous hall and returned to the starting-place while Thjalfi had hardly moved away from it. Then said the delighted king: "It's true, Thjalfi, that you are the fastest human I have ever seen, but you must run faster than that if you are to beat Hugi."

Utgard-Loki then turned to Thor and asked him in what manner he was going to prove himself. Thor threw out his chest and replied that he would contest the prize for the fastest drinker with anyone in the court. Utgard-Loki was mightily pleased and ordered his cup-bearer to bring out his drinking horn. It was massive, even by giant standards. The cup-bearer presented the immense drinking horn to Thor.

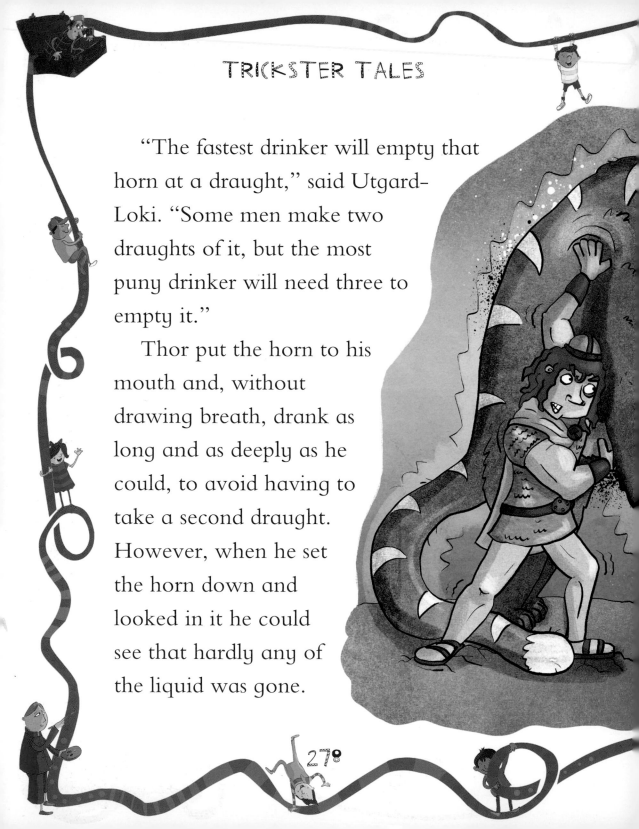

"The fastest drinker will empty that horn at a draught," said Utgard-Loki. "Some men make two draughts of it, but the most puny drinker will need three to empty it."

Thor put the horn to his mouth and, without drawing breath, drank as long and as deeply as he could, to avoid having to take a second draught. However, when he set the horn down and looked in it he could see that hardly any of the liquid was gone.

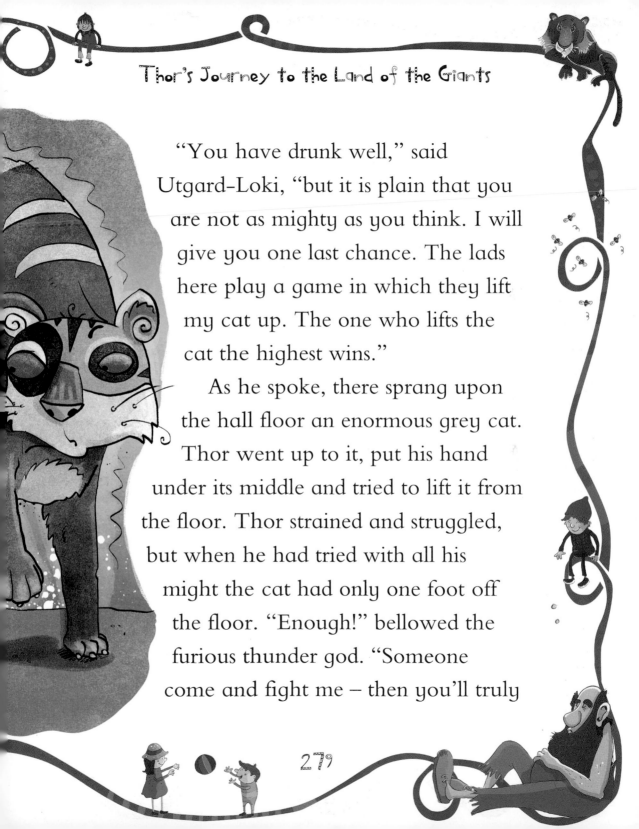

"You have drunk well," said Utgard-Loki, "but it is plain that you are not as mighty as you think. I will give you one last chance. The lads here play a game in which they lift my cat up. The one who lifts the cat the highest wins."

As he spoke, there sprang upon the hall floor an enormous grey cat. Thor went up to it, put his hand under its middle and tried to lift it from the floor. Thor strained and struggled, but when he had tried with all his might the cat had only one foot off the floor. "Enough!" bellowed the furious thunder god. "Someone come and fight me – then you'll truly see how mighty I am!"

The giants all taunted and jeered as Utgard-Loki called forward Elli, a toothless old woman. Burning with humiliation, Thor charged and grappled with her, determined to lay her on the floor in a second and then set to with the giant king himself. But the harder Thor tightened his hold, the firmer the old woman stood. To Thor's horror, he felt himself totter. And at last, after a long tussle, he fell to one knee.

King Utgard-Loki and the giants sprang to their feet and, cheering with gusto, ushered the travellers outside the city wall.

"Now I must tell you the truth," admitted the king, when at last the giants had quietened. "Loki ate fast, but the name

'Logi' means 'flame' – he was eating against fire itself, which consumes everything. Thjalfi ran swiftly – but 'Hugi' means 'thought', which is the swiftest thing in the universe.

"The liquid in my drinking horn was in fact the mighty ocean. You drank so much of it that if I had not seen it with my own eyes, I should never have believed it. You did no less a wondrous thing when you lifted up the cat – which was a magical disguise for the immense Midgard serpent, which circles the world of men.

"Your wrestling match with Elli was, too, a great feat, for she is old age – and no one can defeat old age. Now I want you to leave my city – for now I know how mighty you truly are, I shall never again allow you to enter it."

So Thor was forced to go on his way, never able to forget how he had been the subject of a giant-sized trick.

The Art Contest

A Vietnamese folk tale

Once upon a time – not that long ago – in Southeast Asia, there lived a boy called Trang Quynh. He was thirteen years old and he was the cleverest person in the country of Vietnam. He wasn't the cleverest person in the country of Vietnam by chance. Trang Quynh had worked very hard at it.

As soon as he started school, Trang Quynh had discovered that he really enjoyed reading and he seemed to find remembering things much easier than the other children. He managed to learn all his times tables in just a week, and his classmates were so awed and his teacher so delighted that it spurred him on to memorize more. Soon he had learned the name of every insect and every type of plant in the rainforest, including all the details of their size, colour and medicinal uses.

Next, he learned the whole of *A History of Vietnam* until he could recite it off by heart. He was super-fast at working things out too. He could solve word and picture puzzles in only a second or two, calculate the most complex arithmetic as fast as a computer, and solve the most baffling brainteasers over just a cup of green tea.

It wasn't long before news began to spread of the boy with the super-brain. Day by day, curious neighbours and people from neighbouring towns and villages began to visit Trang Quynh's house, to challenge him with the hardest questions they could think of. Trang Quynh now had to study in the evening and late into the night, in order to continue learning all there was to learn and exercising his brain with new problems.

One day a woman asked him: "How long is the Mekong River?"

"Oh, that's an easy one," the boy replied. Without even having to think, he stated: "It's four thousand, three hundred and fifty kilometres." The boy looked at the woman expectantly. "Well, am I right?" he asked.

"I'm not sure," said the woman, embarrassed. "I don't know the answer myself." And she shuffled away in disgrace.

Up stepped a small child. "What is the capital city of Mexico?" he asked shyly.

"Ah, that's a trick question," Trang Quynh said, wagging his finger, although his eyes were shining with delight. "The capital city of Mexico is Mexico City."

"You'll never guess this riddle," piped up a confident old man. "I have streets but no pavements, I have cities but no buildings, I have forests but no trees, I have rivers yet no water. What am I?"

"Oh, you'll have to do better than that," said Trang Quynh, laughing. "That's a map, of course." And the surrounding crowd clapped and *ooohed* and *aaahed* with wonder and delight.

"I have a big problem," announced a young farmer, "I cannot afford to pay workers to harvest my rice in the fields, so it rots before my family and I can gather all the crops. Can you invent a machine to help us?"

"Leave it with me overnight," said

Trang Quynh, and the next morning he presented the young farmer with a design for a harvesting machine that not only gathered rice twice as quick as any human could, but that also worked by clockwork, so it didn't cost anything to run.

Then one day, a man arrived in the village whom everybody knew to be a genius. He was famous for being an expert on many subjects and accomplished at many different skills. This man said to Trang Quynh, "I can make a drawing of not just one wild animal, but two – in only a minute." He picked up two paintbrushes, one in each hand, dipped them in a saucer of ink, and drew with just a few masterly strokes – *swish swish swish* – the most amazing lion with his right hand and an incredible tiger with his left. "Now," the man said smugly to Trang Quynh, "can you, with your super-brain, top that?"

"Well, I'm not sure," said Trang Quynh, modestly, "but I will do my best." He spread out his ten fingers, dipped them in the ink, and drew them all down the paper at the same time.

"Worms," he announced. "Ten wild animals in one second. I win."

The Valiant Little Tailor

Adapted from a traditional tale
by the Brothers Grimm

There was once a little tailor who was
a very cheeky chap. Maybe he was
cheeky because he was little, I don't know.
In any case, he was little and he was
cheeky and he was a tailor – and that's the
truth of it.

One day, the cheeky little tailor was
sewing and nibbling on a thick slice of
bread and jam (it was strawberry – his

291

favourite) when several big fat flies started buzzing round the jam jar. "Get lost!" he spluttered through a mouthful of crumbs. "Go away! Be off with you!" He flicked at the flies with his sewing, but the stubborn insects just buzzed round the jam jar more determinedly than ever. "I'll show you!" the tailor murmured, and he fetched his broom from the corner.

Very slowly (so as not to arouse the flies' suspicion), he lifted his broom high above his head and – *WHACK!* – brought it down swift and hard on the table. There was no more buzzing. When the cheeky little tailor lifted the broom and saw the seven dead flies underneath, his chest puffed up with pride. "Well, look at that!" he

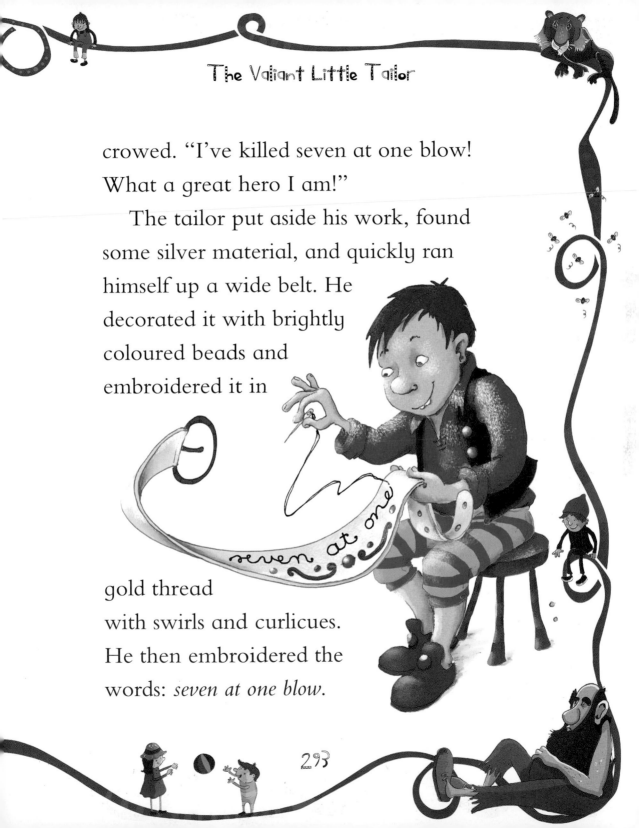

crowed. "I've killed seven at one blow!
What a great hero I am!"

The tailor put aside his work, found
some silver material, and quickly ran
himself up a wide belt. He
decorated it with brightly
coloured beads and
embroidered it in

gold thread
with swirls and curlicues.
He then embroidered the
words: *seven at one blow*.

When it was finished, the tailor buckled the fine belt around his waist and stood in front of the mirror. "My, my!" he breathed. "What's a splendid champion like me doing in a dingy little workroom like this? I should be out and about in public, so everyone can admire me!"

With that, the cheeky little tailor left his house and set off down the road, humming merrily to himself and nodding politely to all he met.

Of course, everyone who bumped into the tailor along the road couldn't help but ask about the marvellous belt he wore. And the cheeky little tailor was only too delighted to explain that it was in honour of his slaying seven attackers with just one blow of his weapon. He told himself it wasn't a lie, exactly. After all, he wasn't actually telling any untruths, he was just missing little bits out – that the seven attackers were actually flies and that his weapon of choice was a broom – and these were just minor details of no real interest to anyone anyway…

It wasn't long before everyone was gossiping about the hero who had killed seven at one blow. "Imagine slaying seven men at just one blow!" people exclaimed.

"No, it wasn't seven men," others insisted, "it was seven trolls!"

"You are wrong," others protested. "It wasn't seven trolls, it was seven dragons!"

Eventually, even the king got to hear of

the very small, but very brave, champion
and he asked him to the palace at once.
The tailor wasn't at all nervous – in fact he
was delighted!

He knocked on the enormous golden
gates and then strode through the mighty
marble halls with his head held high and a
confident swagger, as though he really
was the conquering hero that he
pictured himself to be. When the
cheeky little tailor reached the
throne room, he gave a low, low
bow and then stood
perfectly straight with his
chest puffed out, so
the king could clearly
see and admire the

288

bright, shimmering belt.

"You may rise," the king bade him graciously. "Whoops – I'm sorry, I didn't realize you already had." He gave an embarrassed little cough at his mistake.

"Welcome, mighty champion," he continued, still very surprised at the great hero's small stature. "I was hoping you could help me out with a problem." From his throne, the king looked the cheeky little tailor in the eye. "There are two giants who keep robbing my villages and killing my subjects. If you get rid of them, I'll give you half of my kingdom."

"And…" said the cheeky little tailor (because he was very cheeky like that).

"And what?" said the king, very puzzled.

"And your daughter's hand in marriage," chuckled the tailor. "It's only usual in cases like this."

"Oh very well," grumbled the king. "I'll give you my daughter's hand in marriage as well."

"Very well," chirped the tailor. "Two giants mean nothing to me. Don't forget that I have killed seven at one blow." And with a wink he strode off, his belt sparkling in the sunlight.

When the tailor found the giants, they were both fast asleep under a huge, shady oak tree. The tailor patted his belt comfortingly, picked up two large round pebbles, and tucked them into his shirt. Then he tried to creep up to the tree. He had problems getting close, because each time he walked forward, the giants' enormous snores blew him back.

Finally, he made a mad run for it and – looking a little windswept – reached the trunk. He climbed nimbly into the branches and chuckled to himself. Then he took out one of the stones and dropped it, hitting the first sleeping giant – *plop!* – straight on the nose.

"Oi!" roared the giant, waking up at once and turning on his brother. "What did you do that for, dungbreath?"

"Do what?" mumbled the second giant, half-asleep.

"You know!" bellowed the first giant. "Don't do it again!" And he settled right back down to sleep.

High up in the tree, the cheeky little tailor giggled and dropped his other stone. It bounced right off the first giant's nose.

"Oi!" he boomed, sitting bolt upright and glaring at his brother. "I told you not to do that, thunderpants!" And he socked the second giant right in the face.

"What on earth did you do that for, mouldybeard?" the wounded giant roared, and he punched his brother's arm.

That was the start of a giant fight that raged so long the people in the nearby village thought there was an earthquake. The cheeky little tailor was very nearly shaken out of the oak tree, but at the end of it, the giants both lay dead beneath him

and he had suffered nothing worse than a bruised bottom.

And that is how a tailor came to win half a kingdom and marry a princess – all through being a very cheeky chap. Maybe he was a cheeky chap because he was little, I don't know. In any case, he was little and he was cheeky and he was a tailor – and that's the truth of it.

302

The Never-ending Story

A traditional tale

Once upon a time, there was a village at the edge of a deep, dark forest. None of the villagers ever went into the forest, because they had heard that those who did never came out. No one knew what happened to them – they vanished without a trace. People often told spooky stories of ghosts that lurked in the heart of the forest, where the trees grew closest together and no sunlight could ever be seen. Others told

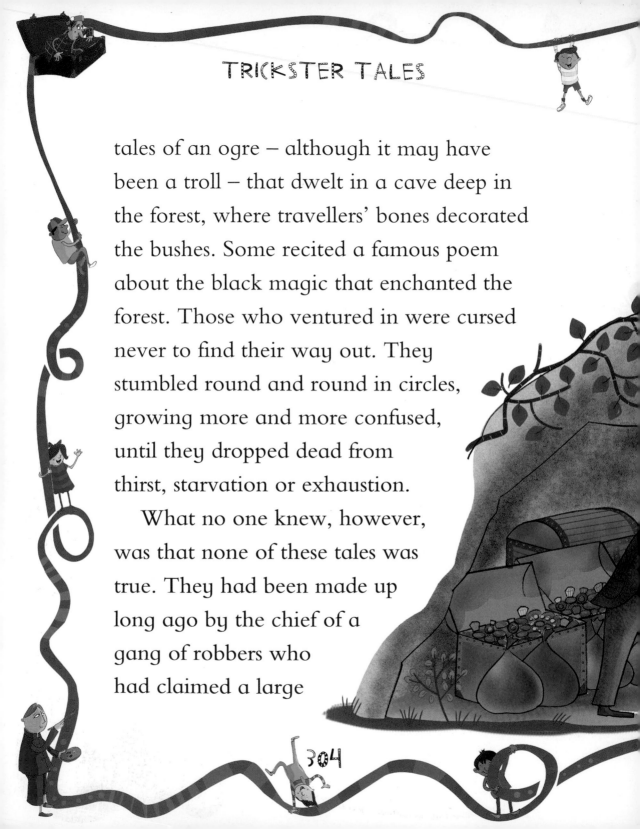

tales of an ogre – although it may have been a troll – that dwelt in a cave deep in the forest, where travellers' bones decorated the bushes. Some recited a famous poem about the black magic that enchanted the forest. Those who ventured in were cursed never to find their way out. They stumbled round and round in circles, growing more and more confused, until they dropped dead from thirst, starvation or exhaustion.

What no one knew, however, was that none of these tales was true. They had been made up long ago by the chief of a gang of robbers who had claimed a large cavern in the forest as a hideout for his gang. He did not want villagers to come traipsing through the trees for a picnic and discover all his stolen gold, jewels and precious treasures. So he invented stories to trick everyone into staying well away.

The stories had done their work better than the robber chief could ever have imagined. And although he had grown old and passed away many years ago, his grandson – who was now the chief – was still never troubled by nosy or bothersome villagers.

So the outlaws had become the most successful gang of bandits for miles around. They could plot and scheme in peace to their hearts' content. Once they had successfully raided, plundered and pillaged, they could disappear into the safety of the forbidden forest, and gloat over their ill-gotten gains without fear of discovery.

In fact, if the robber chief were to tell the truth for once (and he could not remember the last time that he had), he would have to admit that life had become rather dull. There were hardly any challenges for his gang any longer. There was little danger for them and so no accompanying sense of excitement. Something important was missing from their lives – fun. The chief had begun to notice that his robbers had started to argue amongst themselves and fight more than usual – and over the smallest things. He could only put their irritability down to one thing – boredom.

So the chief thought up a cunning plan – a scheme to get his men's hearts pounding, pulses racing and blood pumping. He announced that every night, around the campfire, one of the robbers would tell the others a scary story – one which would strike fear into their hearts. And when the time came when they had each told their story, the robber who was voted to have told the scariest tale would win the enviable position of deputy robber chief.

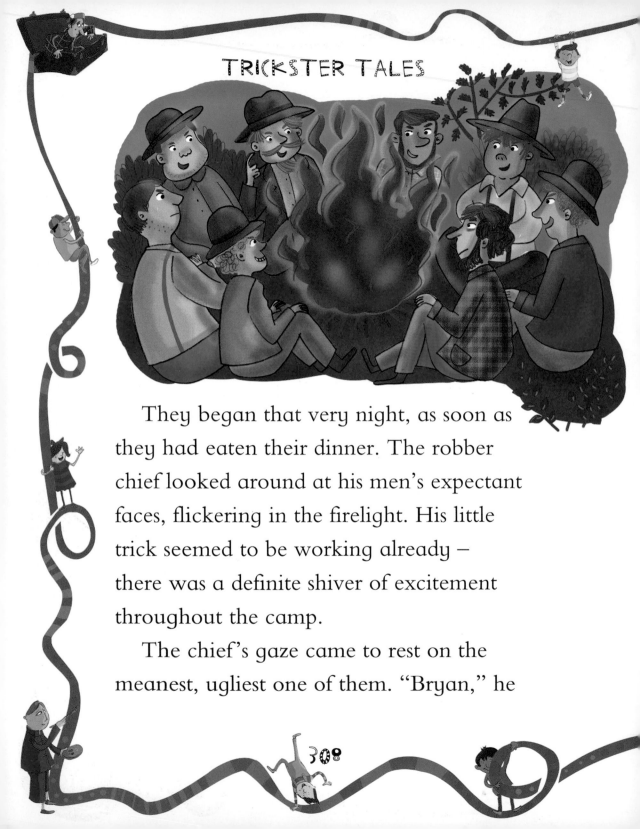

They began that very night, as soon as they had eaten their dinner. The robber chief looked around at his men's expectant faces, flickering in the firelight. His little trick seemed to be working already — there was a definite shiver of excitement throughout the camp.

The chief's gaze came to rest on the meanest, ugliest one of them. "Bryan," he said. "You have the honour of going first. Start us off please – and make it scary!"

Bryan spat out of the corner of his mouth, and said in a hoarse rasp: "Ok boss, I will. Listen up all of you – and listen good, or you'll feel the sting of my blade. My story goes like this:

"Once upon a time, there was a village at the edge of a deep, dark forest. None of the villagers ever went in to the forest, because they had heard that those who did never came out. No one knew what happened to them – they vanished without a trace…"

Crazy Capers

A Mad Tea Party

Adapted from *Alice's Adventures in Wonderland*
by Lewis Carroll

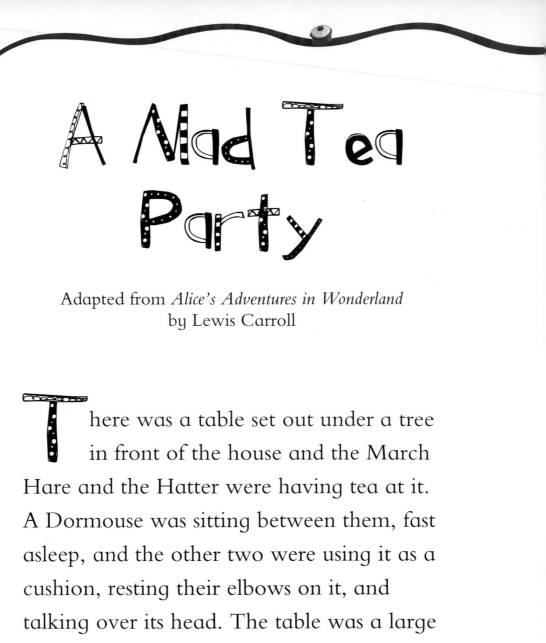

There was a table set out under a tree in front of the house and the March Hare and the Hatter were having tea at it. A Dormouse was sitting between them, fast asleep, and the other two were using it as a cushion, resting their elbows on it, and talking over its head. The table was a large one, but the three were all crowded together at one corner of it. "No room! No

room!" they cried out when they saw
Alice coming.

"There's plenty of room!" said Alice
indignantly, and she sat down in a large
armchair.

"Have some wine," the March Hare
said encouragingly.

Alice looked all round the table, but
there was nothing on it but tea. "I don't see
any wine," she remarked.

"There isn't any," said the March Hare.

"Then it wasn't very civil of you to offer
it," said Alice angrily.

"It wasn't very civil of you to sit down
without being invited," replied the March
Hare sharply.

"I didn't know it was *your* table," said

Alice. "It's laid for a great many more than three."

The Hatter opened his eyes very wide at this, but all he said was, "Why is a raven like a writing-desk?"

'Come, we shall have some fun now!' thought Alice. 'I'm glad they've begun asking riddles.' "I believe I can guess that," she added aloud.

"Do you mean you think you can find out the answer to it?" said the March Hare.

"Exactly so," said Alice.

"Then you should say what you mean," the March Hare went on.

"I do," Alice hastily replied. "At least… I mean what I say – that's the same thing, you know."

"Not the same thing a bit!" said the Hatter. "You might just as well say that 'I see what I eat' is the same thing as 'I eat what I see'!"

"You might just as well say," added the March Hare, "that 'I like what I get' is the same thing as 'I get what I like'!"

"You might just as well say," added the Dormouse, who seemed to be talking in his sleep, "that 'I breathe when I sleep' is the same thing as 'I sleep when I breathe'!"

"It is the same thing with you," said the Hatter. Here the the party sat silent for a minute, while Alice thought over all she could remember about ravens and writing-desks, which wasn't much.

The Hatter was the first to break the

silence. "What day of the month is it?" he said, turning to Alice. He had taken his watch out of his pocket, and was looking at it uneasily, shaking it every now and then, and holding it to his ear.

"The fourth," Alice said.

"Two days wrong!" sighed the Hatter. "I told you butter wouldn't suit the works!" he added angrily to the March Hare.

"It was the best butter," the March Hare meekly replied.

"Some crumbs must have got in as well," the Hatter grumbled. "You shouldn't have put it in with the bread-knife."

The March Hare took the watch and looked at it gloomily. Then he dipped it into his cup of tea and looked at it again.

Alice had been looking over his shoulder with some curiosity. "What a funny watch!" she remarked. "It tells the day of the month and not what o'clock it is!"

"Why should it?" muttered the Hatter. "Does your watch tell you what year it is?"

"Of course not," Alice replied very readily. "But that's because it stays the same year for such a long time together."

"Which is just the case with mine," said the Hatter. Alice felt dreadfully puzzled.

"Have you guessed the riddle yet?" the Hatter said.

"No, I give it up," Alice replied. "What's the answer?"

"I haven't a clue," said the Hatter.

"Nor I," said the March Hare.

Alice sighed wearily. "I think you might do something better with the time," she said, "than waste it in asking riddles that have no answers."

"If you knew Time as well as I do," said the Hatter, "you wouldn't talk about wasting *it*. It's *him*."

"I don't know what you mean," Alice cautiously replied.

"Of course you don't!" the Hatter said, tossing his head. "I dare say you never even spoke to Time! I last saw him in March, at the great concert given by the Queen of Hearts. I had to sing:

'Twinkle, twinkle, little bat!
How I wonder what you're at!

311

Up above the world you fly,
Like a tea-tray in the sky.
Twinkle, twinkle…"'

Here the Dormouse began singing in his sleep, "Twinkle, twinkle, twinkle, twinkle…" and went on so long that they had to pinch him to make him stop.

"Well, I'd hardly finished the first verse," said the Hatter, "when the Queen bawled, 'He's murdering Time! Off with his head!' Ever since, he won't do a thing I ask! It's always six o'clock now."

An idea came to Alice. "Is that why so many tea-things are put out here?" she asked.

"Yes," said the Hatter with a sigh. "It's

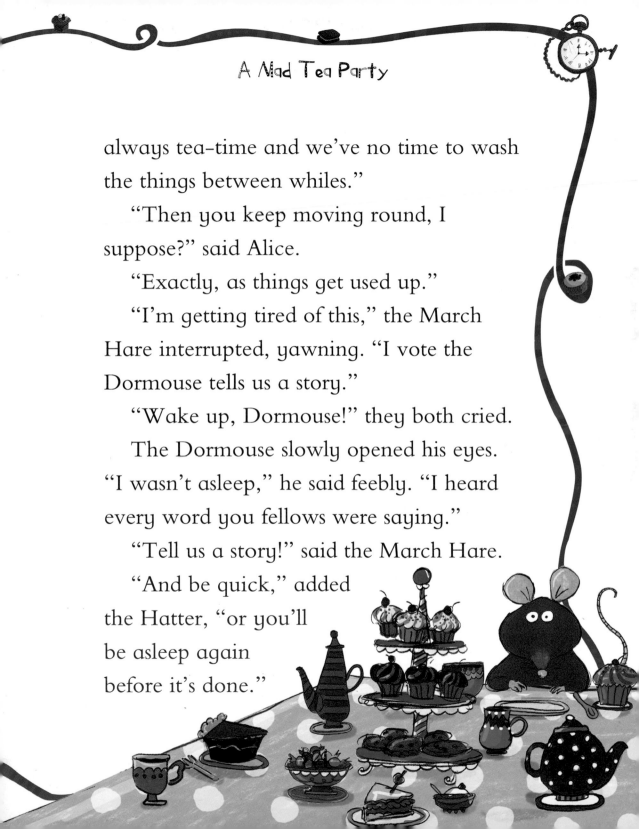

always tea-time and we've no time to wash the things between whiles."

"Then you keep moving round, I suppose?" said Alice.

"Exactly, as things get used up."

"I'm getting tired of this," the March Hare interrupted, yawning. "I vote the Dormouse tells us a story."

"Wake up, Dormouse!" they both cried.

The Dormouse slowly opened his eyes. "I wasn't asleep," he said feebly. "I heard every word you fellows were saying."

"Tell us a story!" said the March Hare.

"And be quick," added the Hatter, "or you'll be asleep again before it's done."

"There were once three little sisters," the Dormouse began in a great hurry. "Their names were Elsie, Lacie and Tillie, and they lived at the bottom of a well…"

"What did they live on?" said Alice.

"They lived on treacle," said the Dormouse, after thinking a minute or two. "It was a treacle-well."

"There's no such thing!" Alice cried.

The Dormouse sulkily remarked, "Finish the story yourself."

"No, please go on!" Alice said very humbly, "I won't interrupt again."

So the Dormouse went on, yawning and rubbing his eyes. "These three little sisters – they were learning to draw…"

"What did they draw?" said Alice, quite

forgetting her promise.

"Treacle," said the Dormouse, without considering at all this time.

"I want a clean cup," interrupted the Hatter. "Let's all move one place on."

He moved on as he spoke, and the Dormouse followed him. The March Hare moved into the Dormouse's place, and Alice rather unwillingly took the place of the March Hare. The Hatter was the only one who got any advantage from the change, and Alice was a good deal worse off than before, as the March Hare had just upset the milk-jug into his plate.

Alice did not wish to offend the Dormouse again, so said very cautiously, "But I don't understand…"

323

"Well then you shouldn't talk," the Hatter declared.

This rudeness was more than Alice could bear. She got up in disgust and walked off. The Dormouse fell asleep instantly, and neither of the others took the least notice of her going, though she looked back once or twice, half hoping they would call after her. The last time she saw them, they were trying to put the Dormouse into the teapot.

"At any rate I'll never go *there* again!" said Alice as she picked her way through the wood. "It's the stupidest tea party I ever was at in all my life!"

Lazy Jack

Adapted from a traditional tale told
by Joseph Jacobs

There was once a young man whose name was Jack, and he lived with his mother on a common. They were very poor. Jack's mother earned a living by spinning, but Jack was lazy and he did nothing but bask in the sun in hot weather and sit by the fire in winter-time. So people called him Lazy Jack. His mother could not get him to do anything for her.

Eventually, one Monday she could stand it no longer. She told him that if he did not begin to work for his porridge, she would have to turn him out to fend for himself.

This brought Jack to his senses, and the very next day he went out and hired himself to a neighbouring farmer for a penny. He laboured all day for his money, but as he was coming home, he lost his hard-earned coin while passing over a brook. "You stupid boy," said his mother, "you should have put it in your pocket."

"I'll make sure I do so next time," replied Jack.

On Wednesday, Jack went out again and hired himself to a cowherd, who gave him a jug of milk for his work. Jack took the jug and put it into the large pocket of his jacket, spilling it all before he got home.

"Dear me," said his old mother. "You should have carried it in your hands."

"I'll make sure I do so next time," replied Jack.

On Thursday Jack hired himself to a cheese-maker, who agreed to give him a cream cheese for his services. In the evening Jack took the cheese, and went home clutching it tight in his hands. By the time he got home the cream cheese had all melted and was dripping between his fingers. "You stupid boy," said his mother, "you should have carried it in a bag."

"I'll make sure I do so next time," replied Jack.

On Friday, Jack again went out and hired himself to a baker, who gave him a large cat for his work. Jack thrust the cat into a bag, threw it over his shoulder, and began striding home. But the furious animal fought so hard to get out of the bag that Jack's back was soon scratched to ribbons, and he was forced to let it go.

When Jack got home, his mother said to him, "You silly fellow, you should have tied a string around its neck and led it along after you."

"I'll make sure I do so next time," replied Jack.

On Saturday, Jack hired himself to a
butcher, who rewarded him with the
handsome present of a shoulder of mutton.
Jack took the mutton, tied a string around
it, and trailed it along after him in the dirt,
so that by the time he had got home the
meat was completely spoiled. His mother
was by this time quite out of patience with
him, for the next day was Sunday, and
now they were going to have to make do
with just cabbage for their dinner.

"You ninney-hammer," she said, "you
should have carried it on your shoulder."

"I'll make sure I do so next time,"
replied Jack.

On the following Monday Jack hired
himself to a shepherd, who gave him a

donkey for his trouble. Jack
found it difficult to hoist
the donkey onto his
shoulders, but at last he did
it, and began walking
slowly home with his prize.

Now it happened that in
the course of his journey he
went past the house of a
rich man, who lived there
with his daughter. She was
a beautiful girl, but could
not hear or speak. She had
never laughed in her life,
and the doctors said she would never
speak till somebody made her laugh.

This young lady happened to be looking

out of the window when Jack
was passing with the donkey
on his shoulders, its legs
sticking up in the air. The
sight was so comical and
strange that she burst out
into a great fit of
laughter – and
immediately
recovered her
speech and
hearing. Her father
was overjoyed, and
immediately ushered
Jack in and offered the
girl's hand in marriage.
Thus Lazy Jack

monkey, he sighed with great relief. "It's only a monkey," he said to himself. "How much mischief can one monkey make?"

If only the Jade Emperor had known!

The monkey was bold and daring, and quickly became king of all the monkeys. After four hundred years, he set his sights higher – he wanted to become immortal, or better still, one of the gods in heaven.

Through many years of hard study, Monkey acquired magic arts. He learned how to change into anything he wanted, to summon a cloud and ride upon it, and – most importantly – the secret of eternal life.

Then, Monkey visited the Dragon King and begged for a magic weapon that befitted his new immortal status. The

Dragon King didn't dare say no to such a powerful creature. He gave Monkey a lethal iron staff, which could shrink to the size of a needle so Monkey could keep it safely in his ear.

Not long afterwards, up in heaven, the Jade Emperor heard a commotion outside the East Gate. His chief minister hurried up to him in a fluster. "Your Imperial Highness, a talking monkey is clamouring to be let into heaven and become a god. He says he knows magic and is immortal – and I'm inclined to believe him, as he's just fought off four guards with an iron staff!"

"Indeed," said the Jade Emperor, stroking his long beard. He thought for a moment and then said: "Well, maybe the

way to stop this monkey causing trouble is
not through force but through wit. Invite
him in and offer him a job. That way, we
can keep an eye on him and make sure he
doesn't go creating havoc."

So the chief minister
hurried back to Monkey

and offered him the position of Supervisor
of the Imperial Stables and Protector of the
Imperial Horses.

"What an important role!" Monkey
exclaimed, very pleased.

However, his delight didn't last long. He
soon discovered that the job consisted
largely of mucking out the stables –
Monkey spent most of every day knee-deep
in dung.

When he realized he had been tricked,
he jumped up and down with rage. "So this
is what the gods think of me, is it?" he
screeched. "Me? The immortal Monkey
King? Well, I won't stand for it!"

He rushed out of the stables,
somersaulted onto a cloud, and sped off to

confront the Jade Emperor.

"Oh magical Monkey," the Jade Emperor soothed, "I apologize if my chief minister offended you. I meant for him to offer you a different position – the Invincible Peerless Guardian of the Garden of the Peaches of Immortality."

"Is that an important job?" the suspicious monkey asked gruffly. "Really?"

"Oh yes, really. Highly important," assured the Jade Emperor.

So Monkey accepted it.

Every day, Monkey stood at the gateway to the Garden of the Peaches of Immortality and kept watch for intruders, his iron staff at the ready. He watched… and watched… and watched… but no one ever came. Nothing ever happened. Monkey just stood there watching the grass and the flowers and the immortal peach trees grow, day after day. How utterly boring it was! After a while, he realized that he had once again been duped. The Jade Emperor was just keeping him out of everyone's way.

"I'll show him what I think of his stupid peaches!" Monkey raged. He charged into the garden, tore down the Peaches of Immortality and ate every last one. Monkey gorged himself until he felt sick, and so he had to lie down and sleep it off.

While he was sleeping, the Jade Emperor came riding up in a chariot to inspect his sacred peaches. He was aghast at what he

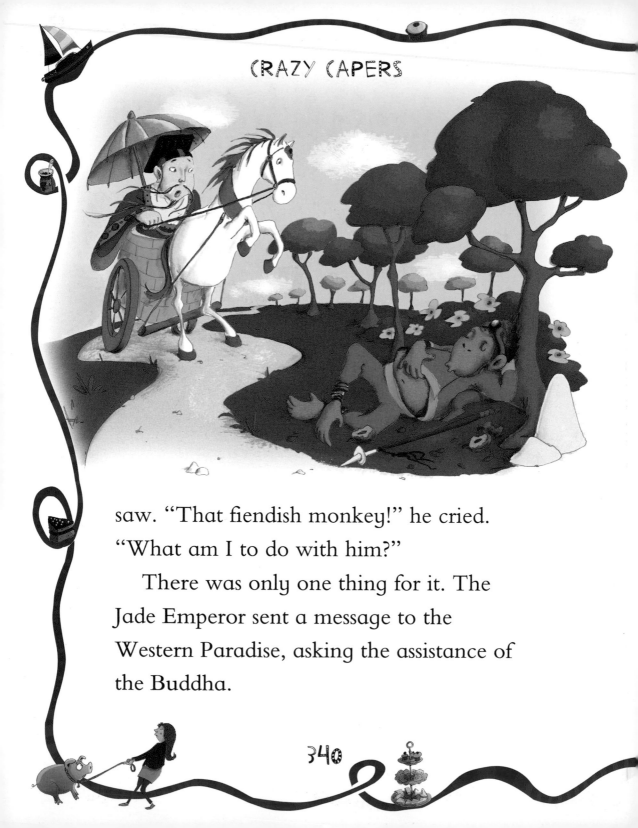

saw. "That fiendish monkey!" he cried.
"What am I to do with him?"

There was only one thing for it. The
Jade Emperor sent a message to the
Western Paradise, asking the assistance of
the Buddha.

So Monkey woke from his stupor to find a huge man wearing a robe, hovering in front of him on a magic cloud.

"Who are you?" cried Monkey rudely.

The man just laughed. "I am the Buddha. I understand you want a high position in heaven."

"Of course!" stated the arrogant monkey. "I have great powers. I have mastered the arts of transformation, cloud-soaring and immortality."

"Indeed," smiled the Buddha. "Well, I am here to teach you the art of humility."

Monkey shrugged. He wasn't sure what 'humility' meant.

"I'll make you a bet," the Buddha said calmly. "If you can jump out of the palm of my hand, the Jade Emperor's throne is yours. But if you cannot, you will return to Earth immediately."

Monkey threw back his head and laughed. "You're on," he said. He shrunk his iron staff and tucked it in his ear, and jumped onto the Buddha's palm. Then he leapt with all his might.

Monkey sped through the air like a bolt of lightning for thousands of miles, until he landed in a place where five olive-coloured pillars reached up into the sky. "This must be the very edge of heaven," he told himself. As proof he had been there, he wrote on the foot of one of the pillars: "Here was Monkey." Then he leapt through the air and landed back in the palm of the Buddha.

"Right, Buddha," ordered Monkey, "go and tell the Jade Emperor I'm in charge now."

"But you've been in my palm the whole time," the Buddha said quietly. "Look down and you'll see."

"What?" scoffed Monkey, looking down indignantly. And there, at the base of the Buddha's middle finger, were the words: "Here was Monkey."

Before Monkey could perform any magic, the Buddha threw him out of heaven. He tumbled through the sky

343

towards Earth, and crashed into a mountainside with such force that he stuck fast in the rock and could not get out.

"You can't do this!" cried Monkey up to heaven. "I'm the Monkey King! I'm immortal! Let me out!" He stopped and thought. Then he added, "Please?"

But it was far too late for good manners. Monkey remained imprisoned in the rock for five hundred years, until the Buddha chose to see if he had learned the art of humility. But that's another story…

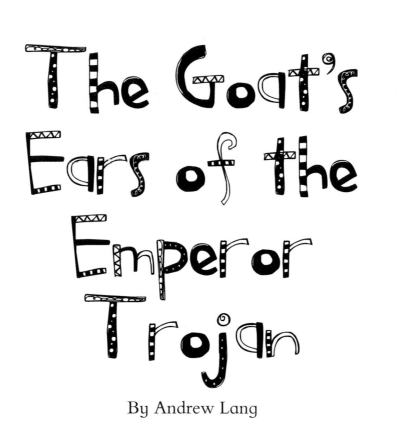

The Goat's Ears of the Emperor Trojan

By Andrew Lang

Once upon a time there lived an emperor whose name was Trojan, and he had ears just like a goat. Every morning, when a barber came to shave him and cut his hair, the emperor asked the barber if he saw anything odd about him. Each barber always replied that the emperor had goat's ears – and was ordered to be put to death.

Now after this state of things had lasted a good while, there was hardly a barber left in the town. The townspeople all talked about it in horrified whispers, wondering why every barber that went up to the palace never returned. Finally the time came when the only qualified barber left was the head barber – the Master of the Company of Barbers. But when he was told it was his turn to go up to the palace he suddenly and mysteriously fell ill and could not go. He ordered one of his apprentices to go in his place.

When the apprentice was taken to the

emperor's bedroom, Trojan demanded to know why his master had not come. The young man replied that his master was ill and had entrusted himself with the honour, which satisfied the emperor. He made himself comfortable as the apprentice put a sheet of fine linen around him.

As the apprentice began his work, he, like all the barbers before him, noticed with dread that the emperor had goat's ears. But when he had finished his work, and the emperor asked if he had noticed anything odd about him, the young man swallowed hard and replied, "No, nothing at all."

The emperor was delighted! He was so pleased that he gave the young apprentice twelve gold coins and declared: "Henceforth you shall come every day to shave me."

So when the apprentice returned home and his master inquired how he had got on with the emperor, the young man answered, "Oh, very well, he says I am to shave him every day, and he gave me these twelve gold coins." But he said nothing about Trojan's goat's ears.

From then on the apprentice went daily

up to the palace, receiving each morning twelve gold coins in payment. But after a while, the secret he had so carefully kept burned within him, and he longed to tell it to somebody. His master saw there was something on his mind and asked what it was. The youth replied that he had been in torment for some months and would never be at ease again until he had shared his secret.

"Well, why not trust me?" said the master barber. "I promise I will keep it to myself. Or, if you prefer, go and tell the priest. If you're not happy with that, go to a faraway field outside the town, dig a hole, whisper the secret into it three times and then bury it."

339

The apprentice liked the sound of the last idea best. So that very afternoon he went to a meadow far outside the town, dug a deep hole, then knelt and whispered into it three times: "The Emperor Trojan has goat's ears." As he said it a great burden seemed to roll off him, and he shovelled the earth carefully back and ran lightly home.

Weeks passed, and there sprang up in the hole an elder tree with three straight stems. Some shepherds, tending their flocks nearby, noticed the tree growing there, and one of them cut off a stem to make a flute out of it. But as soon as he began to play, the flute would do nothing but sing: "The Emperor Trojan has goat's ears."

Of course, it was not long before word spread and the whole town knew of this incredible flute and what it sang – and at last, the news reached the emperor in his palace. Furious, he sent for the apprentice and demanded: "What have you been saying about me to all my people?"

The apprentice tried to defend himself by promising that he had never told anyone what he had seen. But the emperor, instead of listening, drew his sword from its sheath. This so frightened the poor apprentice that he confessed exactly what he had done – how he had whispered the truth three times to the earth, and how in that very place an elder tree had sprung up, and a flute had been cut from it that would only repeat the words he had said.

The emperor ordered his coach to be made ready. He took the youth with him, and they drove to the spot of the elder tree, for he wished to see for himself whether the apprentice's confession was true.

When they reached the tree only one stem was left. The emperor ordered his attendants to cut him a flute from the remaining stem and, when it was ready, his chamberlain began to play on it. But no tune could the chamberlain play, though he was the best flute player in the emperor's court. Nothing came but the words: "The Emperor Trojan has goat's ears."

The emperor then knew that even the earth couldn't help but tell his secret, and

he granted the young man his life –
although he was no longer allowed to be
his barber.

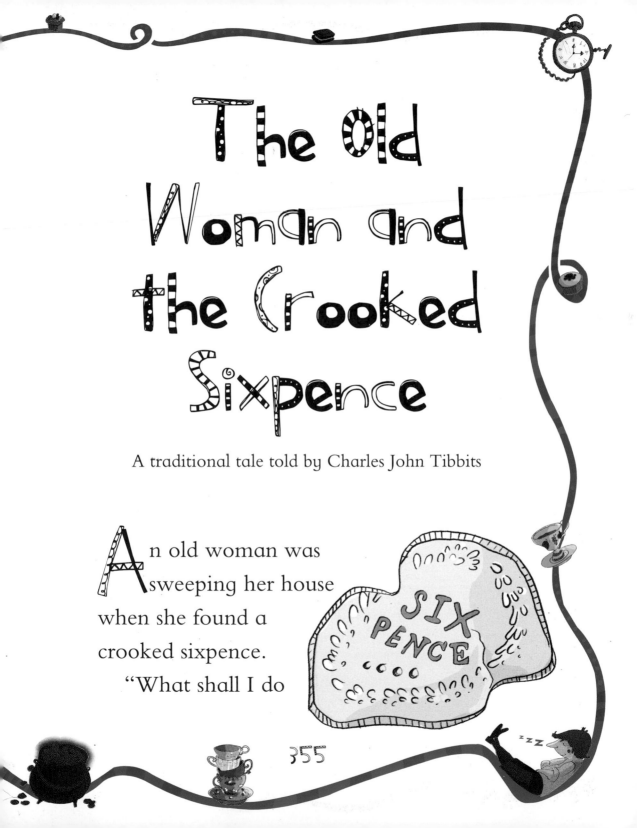

The Old Woman and the Crooked Sixpence

A traditional tale told by Charles John Tibbits

An old woman was sweeping her house when she found a crooked sixpence. "What shall I do

355

with this sixpence?" she said. "I will go to the market and buy a pig with it."

She went, and as she was coming home she came to a stile. Now the pig would not go over the stile. So the woman went on a little further and met a dog.

"Dog," she said, "bite pig. Piggy won't go over the stile, and I shan't get home tonight."

But the dog would not bite the pig. So the woman went on a little further and met a stick.

"Stick," she said, "beat dog. Dog won't bite pig, piggy won't go over the stile, and I shan't get home tonight."

But the stick would not. So the woman went on a little further and met a fire.

"Fire," she said, "burn stick. Stick won't beat dog, dog won't bite pig, piggy won't go over the stile, and I shan't get home tonight."

But the fire would not. So the woman went on a little further, and she met some water.

"Water," she said, "quench fire. Fire won't burn stick, stick won't beat dog, dog won't bite pig, piggy won't go over the stile, and I shan't get home tonight."

But the water would not. So the woman went on a little further and met an ox.

"Ox," she said, "drink water. Water won't quench fire, fire won't burn stick, stick won't beat dog, dog won't bite pig, piggy won't go over the stile, and I shan't

357

get home tonight."

But the ox would not. So the woman went on again, and met a butcher.

"Butcher," she said, "kill ox. Ox won't drink water, water won't quench fire, fire won't burn stick, stick won't beat dog, dog won't bite pig, piggy won't go over the stile, and I shan't get home tonight."

But the butcher would not. The woman went on a little further and met a rope.

"Rope," she said, "hang butcher. Butcher won't kill ox, ox won't drink water, water won't quench fire, fire won't burn stick, stick won't beat dog, dog won't bite pig, piggy won't go over the stile, and I shan't get home tonight."

But the rope would not. Again the

woman went on, and she met a rat.

"Rat," she said, "gnaw rope. Rope won't hang butcher, butcher won't kill ox, ox won't drink water, water won't quench fire, fire won't burn stick, stick won't beat dog, dog won't bite pig, piggy won't go over the stile, and I shan't get home tonight."

But the rat would not. The woman went on a little further and met a cat.

"Cat," she said, "kill rat. Rat won't gnaw rope, rope won't hang butcher, butcher won't kill ox, ox won't drink water, water won't quench fire, fire won't burn stick, stick won't beat dog, dog won't bite pig, piggy won't go over the stile, and I shan't get home tonight."

"Oh," said the cat. "I will kill the rat if you will fetch me some milk from that cow over there."

So the old woman went to the cow and asked her to let her have some milk for the cat.

"No," said the cow, "I won't let you have any milk unless you bring me some hay from that stack over there."

Away went the old woman to the stack and fetched the hay and gave it to the cow. Then the cow gave her some milk, and the old woman took it to the cat.

When the cat had lapped the milk, the cat began to kill the rat, the rat began to gnaw the rope, the rope began to hang the butcher, the butcher began to kill the ox, the ox began to drink the water, the water began to quench the fire, the fire began to burn the stick, the stick began to beat the dog, the dog began to bite the pig, and piggy, in a fright, jumped over the stile. So the old woman got safely home that night.

A Tall Tale

A North American folk tale

"What a big baby!" folk would say to Mrs Bunyan as they peered into the crib at her baby. "He's going to grow up to be a big lad, isn't he?"

But no one could have guessed how fast her son would grow, or how big. After just a week, little Paul was not so little at all and had to wear teenage-sized clothes. His infant lungs were so strong that, when he cried, his wails were so loud he scared all the creatures out of the pond two miles down the lane. After only two weeks, milk would no longer satisfy him. Mrs Bunyan had to give her baby forty bowls of porridge at each feed!

By the time Paul had reached school age, he was bigger and stronger than all the men in town. One morning, the townsfolk were roused from their slumbers by an almighty *BANG!* and the sound of shattering glass. They ran out into the street in their nightclothes, most alarmed, to be greeted by Paul's father waving his hands and crying out: "Don't panic! There's no problem! Paul has just got a slight cold – he sneezed and our windows blew out."

CRAZY CAPERS

No one grumbled about little accidents such as this, as despite his immense height and strength, Paul was a very gentle, likeable fellow. Still, he did find it difficult to make friends with other children, as he was too big to join in with their games. For instance, there's no point in playing tag when your arms and legs are so long that you can reach the other children without even having to run. And making a den in the woods is no fun when you can't fit in it.

So on his tenth birthday, Mr Bunyan bought Paul a pet to keep him company.

And just as Paul was an extraordinary boy, his pet was an extraordinary pet – a bright blue ox named Babe.

From the moment Paul was given Babe they were inseparable and went everywhere together. And no one was all that surprised when Babe grew giant-sized himself. He was so big that a whole barn was needed to house him. It might have been some strange effect that rubbed off on the ox from always being with Paul, or it might have been that Babe was just naturally enormous like his owner – no one was ever sure, but no one was ever bothered either.

Mr and Mrs Bunyan did worry from time to time about what Paul would do to make a living. But they needn't have been concerned. When he grew up, Paul found himself the perfect job as a lumberjack. Now, lumberjacks cut down trees for wood – and in those days wood was used a great deal: to build new homes and make furniture for those homes, to build shops and hotels and churches and jails, to make wagons to carry people and goods, to make sleepers for train tracks, and to make telegraph poles.

Paul set up the biggest and best logging camp in all of North America. He worked with seven other lumberjacks, all over six feet tall, and all called Elmer – so when he called, they all came running. He hired two chefs to cook them pancakes on griddles so huge that they could only grease them by strapping hams on their feet and skating around them. And he filled the lake behind his camp with bubbling pea soup. This way, Paul made sure that his workers were never hungry.

With his team, Paul felled so many trees that in just one week his book-keeper used up more than twenty barrels of ink in recording them all. Paul also fixed the end of the winding road to the logging camp onto Babe's harness, and got the mighty ox to heave and drag the road out straight, so the logs could be taken away more easily.

It's all true, I tell you – no word of a lie! But what most folk say is Paul Bunyan's greatest feat is when he was too tired to pick up his axe as he walked home one evening. By leaving it trailing along the ground as he walked, he carved an enormous cleft in the ground – today known as the Grand Canyon.

So you could say that Paul Bunyan even helped to shape North America.

The Canterville Ghost

Adapted from the story by Oscar Wilde

When Mr Hiram B Otis, the American Minister, bought the mansion at Canterville Chase, everyone told him he was doing a very foolish thing, as there was no doubt at all that the place was haunted. Indeed, Lord Canterville himself said: "I feel bound to tell you, Mr Otis, that the ghost has been seen by several living members of my family, as well as by the rector of the parish. Lady Canterville often got very little sleep at night, in consequence of all the mysterious noises. We have not cared to live in the place since my great-aunt had two skeleton hands placed on her shoulders as she was dressing for dinner."

"My Lord," answered the Minister, "I come from a modern country where we have everything that money can buy. I believe that if there were such things as ghosts in Europe, we'd have had them at home in America by now, in one of our public museums, or on the road as a show."

"Well, if you don't mind a ghost in the house, then that's alright," said

Lord Canterville, smiling. "Only you must remember that I warned you."

A few weeks later, the sale was finalized and the Minister travelled to Canterville Chase with his family: Mrs Otis, their eldest son Washington, fifteen-year-old Miss Virginia E Otis, and the twins – delightful boys. The railway station was seven miles from Canterville Chase, so Mr Otis had telegraphed for a waggonette to meet them. It was a lovely July evening and they drove along in high spirits. However, as they entered the grounds of Canterville Chase, the sky became suddenly overcast, a great crowd of rooks passed silently over their heads, and big drops of rain began to fall.

Standing on the steps to receive them was old Mrs Umney, the housekeeper. She made them each a low curtsey as they alighted, and said in a quaint, old-fashioned manner, "I bid you welcome to Canterville Chase." Following her, they passed through the fine Tudor hallway and the library and were shown in to the dining room.

At eleven o'clock the family retired to their rooms and by half past all the lights were out. Some time after, Mr Otis was awakened by a curious noise in the corridor, just outside his room. It sounded like the clank of metal, and with it he distinctly heard the sound of footsteps. He put on his slippers, took a small oblong

phial out of his suitcase, and opened
the door. Right in front of him he
saw, in the pale moonlight, the ghost
of an old man. Long white hair fell
over his shoulders in matted coils,
his old-fashioned garments were
ragged, and from his wrists and
ankles hung heavy manacles.

"My dear sir," said Mr Otis,
"I really must insist on your oiling
those noisy chains, and have brought
you for that purpose a small bottle of
Tammany Rising Sun Oil. It is said to be
completely effective upon one application."
With these words, the American Minister
laid the bottle down on a nearby table, and
retired to his room.

For a moment the Canterville ghost stood quite motionless in indignation. Then he turned and fled down the corridor, uttering hollow groans and emitting a ghastly pale glow. However, as he reached the top of the great oak staircase, a door was flung open, two little white-robed figures appeared, and a large pillow whizzed past his head!

CRAZY CAPERS

The ghost hastily vanished through the wall and made for a secret chamber in the left wing, where he recovered his breath. Never, in a brilliant and uninterrupted haunting career of three hundred years, had he been so grossly insulted. In fact, no ghost that he knew of in history had ever been treated in this manner! Accordingly, he determined to have vengeance.

A few nights later, shortly after the Otis family had gone to bed, they were suddenly startled by the Canterville ghost's best spooky laugh, coming from the landing. The twins dashed towards the stairs and shot their pea-shooters at him, before Mrs Otis appeared in a light blue dressing gown. "I am afraid you sound far from well," she said, "so I've brought you a bottle of Dr Dobell's cough mixture. If it is a sore throat, you will find it a most excellent remedy." The ghost glared at her in irritation, became faintly phosphorescent, then vanished with a churchyard groan.

By the time the ghost reached his room, he was most agitated. The Otis family were really extremely annoying!

For his third attempt to frighten the American Minister and his family he selected Friday, 13 August for his appearance and chose to wear a large slouched hat with a red feather, a winding-sheet frilled at the wrists and neck, and a rusty dagger. At half past midnight, he glided down the passage that led to luckless

THE OTIS GHOST, THE ONLY REAL SPOOK!

Washington's room. He turned the corner, but then fell back with a piteous wail of terror. Right in front of him stood another ghost – it was motionless, but terrible. It had a round orange face stretched in a horrible jagged grin, and its body was swathed in a white sheet. On its chest was a placard with strange black writing. The terrified spectre fled back to his room and didn't dare return to read the placard till the light of morning. "THE OTIS GHOST," it read, "THE ONLY REAL SPOOK!"

The Canterville ghost couldn't believe it. Those wicked Otis children were mocking him. He suddenly felt very weak and tired, and retired to his room for five days.

However, he had no choice but to fulfil his ghostly obligations. So for the next three Saturdays, he dutifully traversed the corridor at night – although he took every possible precaution against being either heard or seen. He glided as lightly as possible, wore a large black velvet cloak, and was careful to use the Rising Sun Oil on his chains.

Still, in spite of all this, he was not left untormented. Strings were continually being stretched across the corridor, over which he tripped in the dark. One night, a big heavy jug of cold water fell right on him – it would have wetted him to the skin if he had any – while stifled shrieks of laughter could be heard from a nearby bedroom. Another night, two figures suddenly leapt out on him from a dark corner, waving their arms wildly above their heads and delightedly shrieking "BOO!" at him.

After this, the Canterville ghost

disappeared. The twins lay in wait for him on several occasions, but to no avail. It was generally assumed that the ghost had gone away. In fact, Mr Otis wrote a letter to that effect to Lord Canterville, who in reply expressed his great pleasure at the news, and sent his best congratulations.

The Otises, however, were deceived, for the Canterville ghost remained in the house, though he was now little more than an invalid.

One evening, Virginia was running past the Tapestry Chamber, the door of which happened to be open, when to her immense surprise she noticed the Canterville ghost sitting by the window. He was staring gloomily out at the garden, watching the gold and red autumn leaves dancing through the air. His head was leaning on his hand, and even for a ghost he looked mournful. Virginia was filled with pity.

"I am sorry for you," she whispered.

The ghost looked round in astonishment

at the girl. "Please don't go, Miss Virginia," he cried, "I am so lonely, and I really don't know what to do. I am tired of endless haunting – I want to sleep and I cannot."

"Why," said the puzzled young girl, "you merely have to go to bed and shut your eyes. Even babies know how to do that, and they are not very clever."

"I have not slept for three hundred years," he said sadly, and Virginia's blue eyes widened in surprise. "I am so tired."

Virginia came towards him, and kneeling down at his side, looked up into his withered face.

"Poor ghost," she murmured, "you mean you want the sleep of death?"

"Yes," sighed the ghost with a small

373

sniff. "How wonderful it must be to be at peace… But you can help me, you know. Have you ever read the old prophecy inscribed on the library window? It says:

'When a golden girl can win
Prayer from out the lips of sin,
When a child gives up its tears
And the barren almond bears,
Then shall all the house be still
And peace come to Canterville.'

"The lines mean that you must pray with me and cry for me, and then the Angel of Death may have mercy on me."

Virginia met the ghost's gaze. "I am not afraid," she said firmly. "I want to help."

A look of joy spread across the ghost's face, and he took Virginia's hand. His fingers were as cold as ice, but Virginia did not falter. Together, the two began to pray, and as they did so, Virginia felt so terribly sorry for the ghost that her tears began to fall. They blurred her eyes so she did not see when he faded away and disappeared. But afterwards, when she went to the window and gazed out, she noticed that the withered almond tree in the garden had blossomed. She could see the flowers quite plainly in the moonlight, a parting gift from the funny old Canterville ghost.

The Unintentional Adventures of Wali Dad

Adapted from an Indian and Pakistani
folk tale told by Andrew Lang

Once upon a time there lived a poor old
man named Wali Dad who lived by
himself in a mud hut on the outskirts of
town. Every day, Wali Dad cut and
bundled wild grass, which he sold as animal

feed. And every day, the old grass-cutter earned three pennies. He spent one penny on food, one penny on clothes and any other needs, and he saved one penny in a pot he kept under the floor of his hut.

Wali Dad lived happily in this way for many years, until one evening he realized that his pot was full to bursting. "Whatever am I going to do with all this money?" he murmured to himself. "I have everything I need. Nothing I could buy would make my life happier."

Next day, Wali Dad staggered with his pot to a jeweller's shop and spent all his money on a beautiful gold bracelet. Then he visited a rich merchant friend.

"Please will you do something for me?"

Wali Dad asked. "I have heard that the princess of Khaistan is incredibly beautiful, but also clever and kind-hearted. Next time you're passing that way, please take her this bracelet, with my compliments."

The merchant was surprised, but did as Wali Dad had asked. The princess was so delighted that she insisted on sending a gift back in return…

When Wali Dad saw the merchant arriving at his hut with a camel-load of fine silks, his face fell. "What's this you're bringing me?" he asked. "I can't do anything with this costly stuff! Do you know anyone who might want it?"

"Well…" considered the merchant, "the prince of Nekabad is a very noble man. I am sure he would put it to good use."

"That's that then," replied Wali Dad.

On the merchant's next journey to Nekabad, he gave the silk to the prince. And a few months later, the merchant returned to Wali Dad's hut with twelve fine horses, in gratitude from the prince.

CRAZY CAPERS

"Oh no!" groaned Wali Dad, looking at the stamping steeds. "What am I meant to do with these fine beasts? I'll tell you what, keep two for yourself and take the rest to that nice princess in Khaistan."

The merchant went off once more, chuckling to himself.

The princess was flattered, but also baffled, at the gift of the horses. "Who is this Wali Dad? And why does he keep sending me gifts?" she asked her father, out of earshot of the merchant.

"If it's making you uncomfortable," the king advised her, "then discourage him. Send him a gift so luxurious that he cannot possibly match it, and he will stop."

So the merchant returned to Wali Dad's

little hut with twenty mules loaded with sacks of silver.

"Oh my goodness!" cried Wali Dad, his eyes wide with horror. "I have no need for this — and the silver will attract robbers from miles around! Please do me a kindness and take them away!" he begged the merchant. "Keep two mules and their loads for yourself, and take the rest to that noble prince in Nekabad."

But when the prince received the eighteen mules and their sacks of silver he was just as baffled as the princess. Upon consulting his father, he received the same advice. Which is why the merchant presently found himself returning to Wali Dad's hut with twenty horses wearing

381

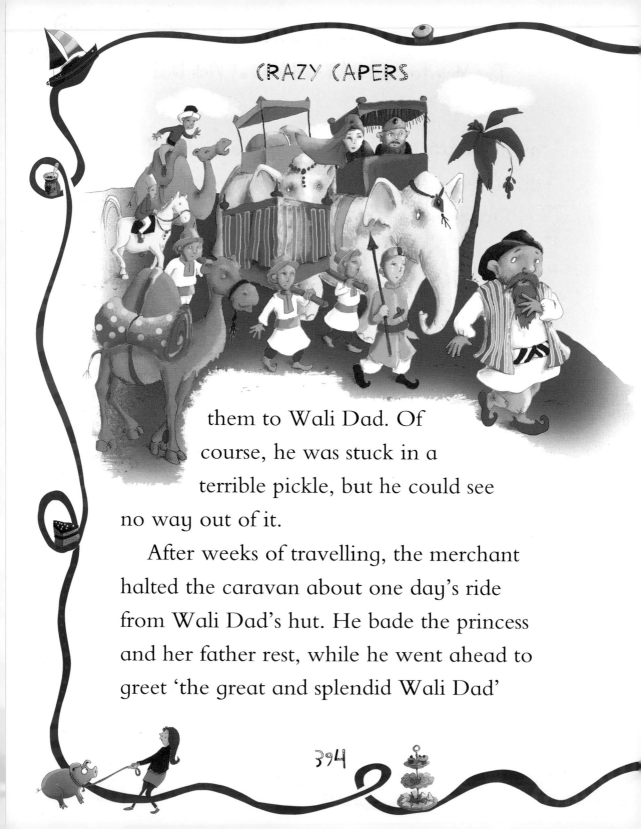

them to Wali Dad. Of
course, he was stuck in a
terrible pickle, but he could see
no way out of it.

After weeks of travelling, the merchant
halted the caravan about one day's ride
from Wali Dad's hut. He bade the princess
and her father rest, while he went ahead to
greet 'the great and splendid Wali Dad'

and seek an interview.

Of course, Wali Dad fell on his knees and wailed at the news. "I am sorry, I am sorry!" he sobbed to the merchant. "I have brought shame upon the princess and disaster upon us both." And the merchant trudged back to the caravan, hanging his head in despair.

Before sunrise next morning, Wali Dad left his little hut. He could see no other way out of his predicament than to travel far, far away, where he could never be found.

The old man hadn't gone far down the road when he was stopped by a stranger coming the opposite way, who shimmered strangely in the dawn light. "Your pure heart will be rewarded," the mysterious stranger told Wali Dad. "Go home. Everything will be alright."

At this, Wali Dad felt suddenly calm. As he turned back, he noticed that instead of his plain rags, he was now clothed in jewelled robes. And where his little hut should have been standing there now stood a splendid palace.

When the merchant arrived with the caravan and found Wali Dad wearing fine garments, sitting in beautiful gardens amid splendid marble halls, he could not believe his eyes. While the princess and king of Khaistan were utterly charmed by Wali Dad's simple conversation and good nature, the merchant felt sure he must be dreaming. And when a second caravan arrived at the

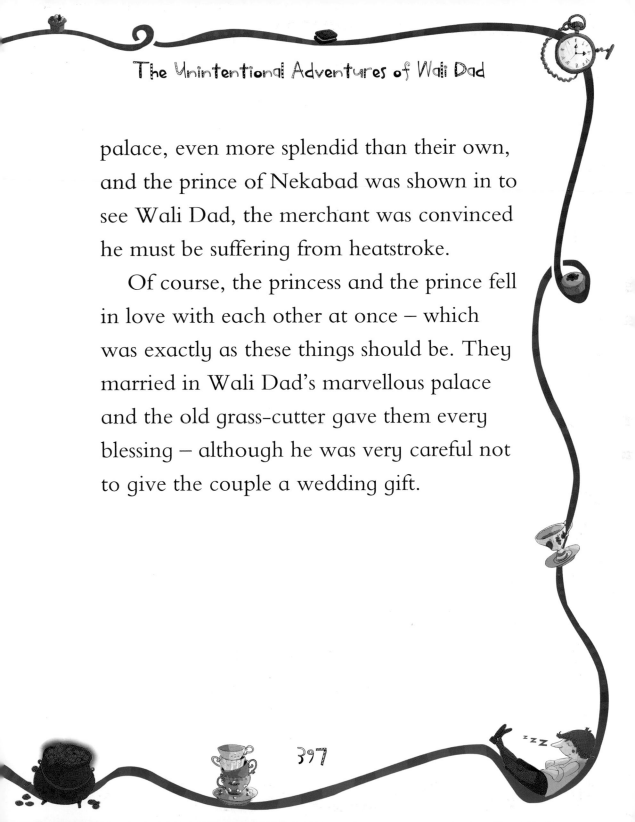

palace, even more splendid than their own, and the prince of Nekabad was shown in to see Wali Dad, the merchant was convinced he must be suffering from heatstroke.

Of course, the princess and the prince fell in love with each other at once – which was exactly as these things should be. They married in Wali Dad's marvellous palace and the old grass-cutter gave them every blessing – although he was very careful not to give the couple a wedding gift.

Sir Gammer Vans' Strange Story

A folk tale told by Joseph Jacobs

Last Sunday morning at six o'clock in the evening, as I was sailing over the tops of the mountains in my little boat, I met two men on horseback riding on one mare. I asked them, "Can you tell me whether the little old woman is dead yet who was hanged last Saturday week for drowning herself in a shower of feathers?"

They said they could not positively inform me, but if I went to Sir Gammer Vans he could tell me all about it. "But how am I to know the house?" I asked.

"Ho, it is easy enough," said they, "for it is a brick house, built entirely of flints, standing alone by itself in the middle of sixty or seventy others just like it."

"Oh, nothing in the world is easier, then," said I.

"Nothing can be easier," said they, so I went on my way.

Now this Sir Gammer Vans was a giant, and a bottle-maker. And as all giants who are bottle-makers usually pop out of a little thumb-bottle from behind the door, so did Sir Gammer Vans.

"How d'ye do?" says he.

"Very well, I thank you," says I.

"Have some breakfast with me?"

"With all my heart," says I.

So he gave me a slice of beer and a cup of cold veal, and the little dog under the table picked up all the crumbs.

"Tie him up," says I.

"No, don't tie him up," says he, "for he killed a hare yesterday. And if you don't believe me, I'll show you the hare alive in a basket."

So he took me into his garden to show me the curiosities. In one corner there was a fox hatching eagle's eggs. In another, there was an iron apple tree, entirely

covered with pears and lead. In the third corner, there was the hare that the dog killed yesterday, alive in the basket. And in the fourth was the little dog passing by.

Sir Gammer Vans took me into the park to show me his deer. I remembered that I had a warrant in my pocket to shoot deer for His Majesty's dinner, so I set fire to my bow, poised my arrow, and shot among them. I lost my arrow – however, upon searching I found it again in the hollow of a tree. I felt it – it felt clammy. I smelt it – it smelt of honey.

"Oh, ho," I said, "here's a bees' nest," and from out of the hollow sprang a covey of partridges. So I shot at them too.

Some say I killed eighteen, but I am sure

I killed thirty-six – besides a dead salmon that was flying over the bridge, of which I made the best apple-pie I ever tasted.

The First Moccasins

A Native American traditional tale

Long ago, a tribe on the Great Plains had a mighty warrior chief. But he had one weakness – extremely sore feet. All the tribespeople went barefoot, running swift as hares through the long grasses. But none of them suffered with sore feet like the chief. His feet were always red and rubbed raw, with torn and tattered toenails. The chief knew that other tribes laughed at him behind his back. And when he caught some of the children in his own tribe pointing and sniggering, he'd had enough! He ordered his medicine man to find an answer – or else.

The fearful medicine man thought of a plan. He commanded the tribeswomen to gather lots of reeds, and with them weave a long, narrow mat. Then he appointed four braves to roll the mat out in front of the chief whenever he wanted to go anywhere, so he could walk on it.

When the medicine man demonstrated his idea, the chief grunted, "Humph!" and hid a smile.

It worked reasonably well for a while. But whenever the length of mat ran out, and the chief had to wait for the four

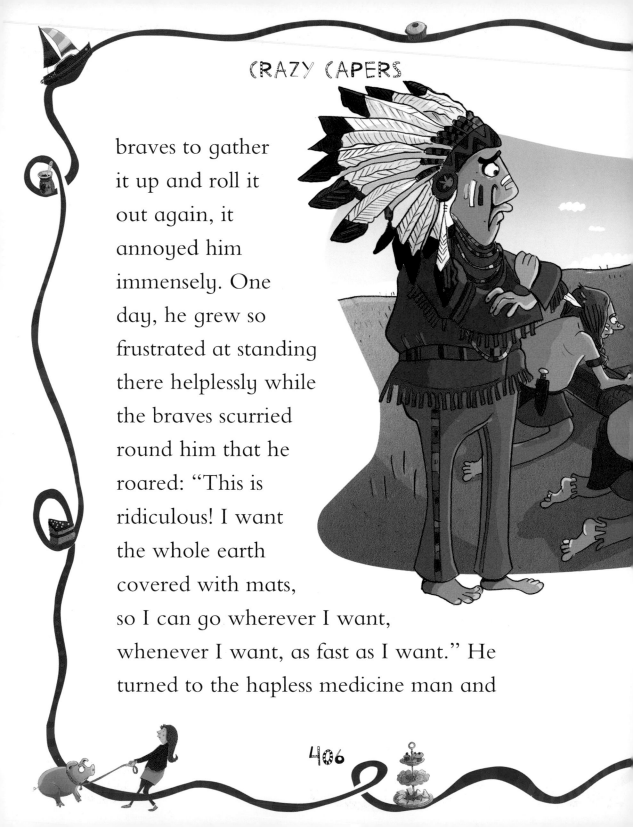

braves to gather it up and roll it out again, it annoyed him immensely. One day, he grew so frustrated at standing there helplessly while the braves scurried round him that he roared: "This is ridiculous! I want the whole earth covered with mats, so I can go wherever I want, whenever I want, as fast as I want." He turned to the hapless medicine man and ordered: "Have it done by the full moon – or else!" Then he strode back to his teepee and would not be coaxed out. The medicine man asked the tribeswomen to prepare animal skins at top speed and commanded every last brave to help spread them out over the earth. And the day before the full moon, the medicine man went nervously to the chief's teepee and told him it was done.

"Humph!" grunted the chief and hid a

smile. He stepped out of his teepee and surveyed the skins covering the earth in all directions, as far as he could see. He called for a hunt the very next day, so he could enjoy running as fast and as far as he liked.

Of course, it was impossible for the skins to cover the earth entirely. The swift-footed chief didn't notice where the skins finished, and stepped straight into a patch of thorns. He howled with pain and rage.

Back in the village, the furious chief raged at his unfortunate medicine man: "You have failed me. Tomorrow you will meet your fate."

But by morning, the desperate medicine man had come up with his best idea yet – he had made what looked like two small leather canoes. Trembling, he knelt before the chief and eased them over his feet.

They felt snug. They felt warm. They felt comfortable.

Suddenly, the chief got the idea.

"Humph!" he grunted and hid a smile as he stood up. He took one step. Then another. Then he strode away, beaming.

And from that day onwards, all the Native American people wore moccasins.

Absurd Accidents

How the Camel got his Hump

Adapted from the story by Rudyard Kipling

In the beginning of years, when the world was so new and all, and the Animals were just beginning to work for Man, there was a Camel. He lived in the middle of a Howling Desert and he did not want to work. So he ate sticks and thorns and tamarisks and milkweed and prickles, most 'scruciating idle, and when anybody spoke to him he said "Humph!" Just "Humph!" and no more.

Presently the Horse came to him on Monday morning, with a saddle on his back and a bit in his mouth, and said, "Camel, O Camel, come out and trot like the rest of us."

"Humph!" said the Camel, and the Horse went away and told the Man.

Presently the Dog came to him with a stick in his mouth, and said, "Camel, O Camel, come and fetch and carry like the rest of us."

"Humph!" said the Camel, and the Dog went away and told the Man.

Presently the Ox came to him, with the yoke on his neck and said, "Camel, O Camel, come out and plough like the rest of us."

"Humph!" said the Camel, and the Ox went away and told the Man.

At the end of the day the Man called the Horse and the Dog and the Ox together, and said, "Three, O Three, I'm very sorry for you (with the world so new-and-all), but that Humph-thing in the Desert can't work or he would have been here by now, so I am going to leave him alone, and you must work double-time to make up for it."

That made the Three very angry (with the world so new-and-all), and they held a pow-wow on the edge of the Desert. The Camel came along chewing on milkweed most 'scruciating idle, and laughed at them. Then he said "Humph!" and went away again.

Presently there came along the Djinn in charge of All Deserts, in a rolling cloud of dust (Djinns always travel that way because it is Magic), and he stopped to pow-wow with the Three.

"Djinn of All Deserts," said the Horse, "is it right for anyone to be idle, with the world so new-and-all?"

"Certainly not," said the Djinn.

"Well," said the Horse, "there's a thing in the middle of your Howling Desert with a long neck and long legs, and he hasn't done a stroke of work since Monday morning. He won't trot."

"Whew!" said the Djinn, whistling. "That's my Camel, for all the gold in Arabia! What does he say about it?"

"He says 'Humph!'" said the Dog. "And he won't fetch and carry."

"Does he say anything else?"

"Only 'Humph!' – and he won't plough," said the Ox.

"Very good," said the Djinn. "I'll 'humph' him, if you will kindly wait just a minute."

The Djinn rolled himself up in his dust-cloak and took a bearing across the desert, and found the Camel most 'scruciatingly idle, looking at his own reflection in a pool of water.

"My long and bubbling friend," said the Djinn, "what's this I hear of your doing no work, with the world so new-and-all?"

"Humph!" said the Camel.

The Djinn sat down with his chin in his hand, and began to think a Great Magic, while the Camel looked at his own reflection in the pool of water.

"You've given the Three extra work ever since Monday morning, all on account of your 'scruciating idleness," said the Djinn, and with his chin in his hand he went on thinking Magics.

"Humph!" said the Camel.

"I shouldn't say that again if I were you," said the Djinn. "Bubbles, I want you to work."

The Camel said "Humph!" again. No sooner had he said it than he saw his smooth back, which he was so proud of, puffing up and puffing up into a great big lolloping humph.

"Do you see that?" said the Djinn. "That's your very own humph that you've brought upon your very own self by not working. Today is Thursday, and you've done no work since Monday, when the work began. Now you are going to work."

"How can I," said the Camel, "with this

418

humph on my back?"

"That has a purpose," said the Djinn, "all because you missed those three days. You will be able to work now for three days without eating, because you can live off your humph – and don't you ever say I never did anything for you. Come out of the Desert and go to the Three, and behave. Humph yourself!"

So, humph and all, the Camel humphed himself away to join the Three. And from that day to this the Camel always wears a humph – although we call it a 'hump' now, so we don't hurt his feelings.

The Three Wishes

Adapted from an English folk tale
told by Joseph Jacobs

Once upon a time – and to be sure it was a long time ago – there lived a poor woodman in a great forest. Every day of his life he went out to fell timber. One day, before he started out, his wife filled his wallet and slung his bottle on his back, that he might have meat and drink for the day. He had marked out a huge old oak that he thought he could chop into a good many logs. When he reached it, he took his axe and swung it round his head to fell the tree at one stroke. But suddenly, there stood before him a fairy who begged and pleaded with him to spare the tree. The woodman was dazed with wonder and couldn't utter a word. When he found his tongue at last, he replied, "Well, I'll do as you ask."

"Thank you most sincerely," said the fairy. "To show you how grateful I am, I'll grant you your next three wishes, whatever they may be." With that, the fairy vanished.

At the day's end, the woodman slung his wallet and bottle over his shoulder and started for home. The journey was long, but all the way, the poor man remained stunned by the strange thing that had befallen him. When he got home there was nothing in his head but the wish to sit down and rest. He sank into an armchair by the blazing fire.

"Isn't my supper ready yet?" he said to his wife.

"Not for a couple of hours," she said.

"Ah!" groaned the woodman. "I wish I'd a good link of black pudding here before me."

No sooner had he said it than – *clatter, clatter, rustle, rustle* – what should come down the chimney but a link of the very finest black pudding.

"What's all this?" squawked his wife.

Then the woodman remembered the

fairy and told his wife what had happened.

"Oh, you are a fool!" she cried. "I wish the pudding were on your nose, I do!"

And before you could say 'Jack Robinson', the link of black pudding was stuck to the woodman's nose. He gave a pull but it held fast, and his wife gave a pull but still it held, and they both pulled till they had nearly pulled the woodman's nose off, but the black pudding was stuck fast.

"Whatever shall we do now?" he said.

"I suppose it doesn't look that bad…" she said, trying to make him feel better.

424

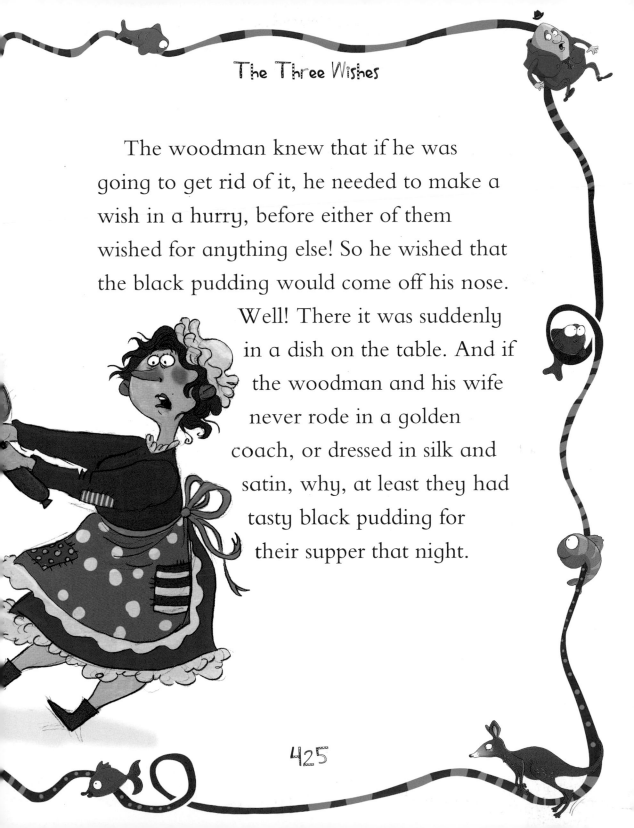

The woodman knew that if he was
going to get rid of it, he needed to make a
wish in a hurry, before either of them
wished for anything else! So he wished that
the black pudding would come off his nose.

Well! There it was suddenly
in a dish on the table. And if
the woodman and his wife
never rode in a golden
coach, or dressed in silk and
satin, why, at least they had
tasty black pudding for
their supper that night.

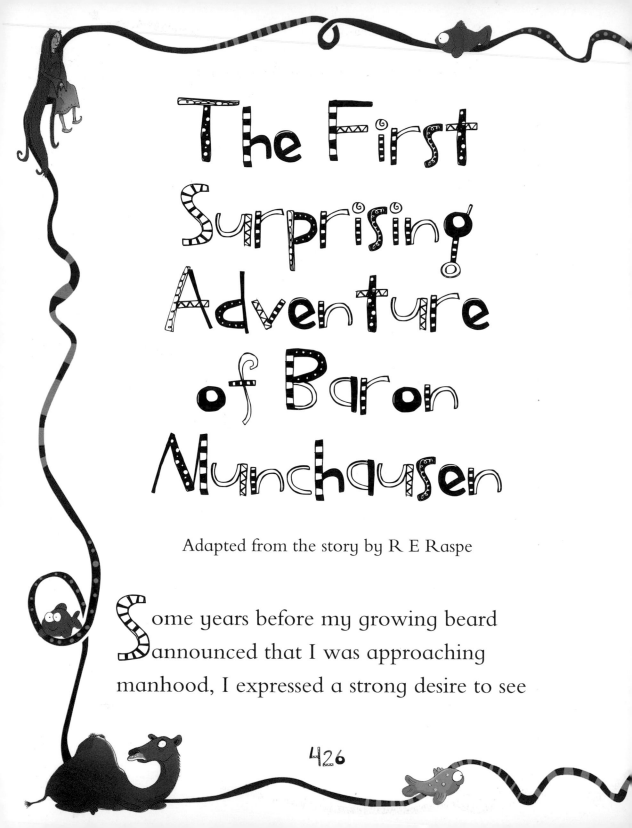

The First Surprising Adventure of Baron Munchausen

Adapted from the story by R E Raspe

Some years before my growing beard announced that I was approaching manhood, I expressed a strong desire to see

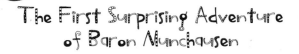

the world. My father agreed for me to accompany a cousin on a voyage to the island of Ceylon, where his uncle had lived as a governor for many years.

We sailed from Amsterdam. The only circumstance that happened on our voyage that is worth relating was that, on an island where we anchored to take in wood and water, a violent storm tore up by the roots a great number of trees of enormous bulk and height. Some of these trees weighed many tonnes, yet they were carried by the wind so amazingly high that they resembled bird feathers floating in the air, for they were at least five miles above the earth. However, as soon as the storm subsided they all fell straight back down

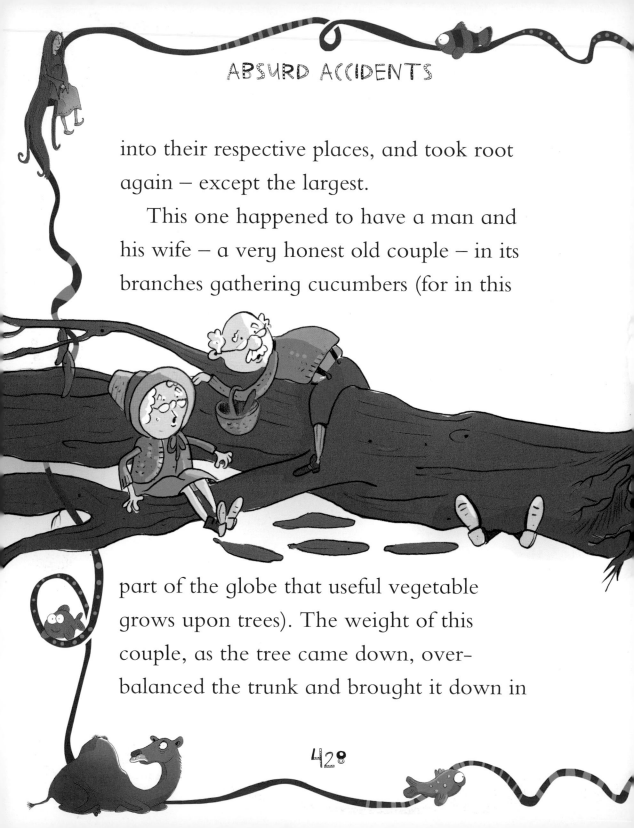

into their respective places, and took root again — except the largest.

This one happened to have a man and his wife — a very honest old couple — in its branches gathering cucumbers (for in this part of the globe that useful vegetable grows upon trees). The weight of this couple, as the tree came down, over-balanced the trunk and brought it down in

a horizontal position. It fell upon the chief-
man of the island and killed him on the
spot, whereupon the people chose the
cucumber-gatherers who had fallen from
the sky as their new chiefs.

After we had repaired the damages
our vessel sustained in this remarkable
storm, we sailed with a fair wind for
the object of our voyage.

In about six weeks we arrived at
Ceylon, where we were received with
great marks of friendship and true
politeness. After we had been there
about a fortnight, I accompanied one
of the governor's brothers upon a
shooting expedition.

We headed into the countryside, but the

man was fitter than me and more used to the heat, so he quickly left me behind. I had followed in his tracks to the banks of a broad river, when I thought I heard a rustling noise behind me.

On turning about I was petrified to see a lion approaching, evidently with the intention of eating me! What could I do? My gun was only loaded with tiny pellets for shooting birds, and I had no other bullets with me. I fired anyway, hoping to wound or even frighten the beast – but the sound just enraged him, for with a mighty bound he came charging at me!

I turned and attempted to escape, but that only added to my distress – for I nearly tripped over a large crocodile who had his

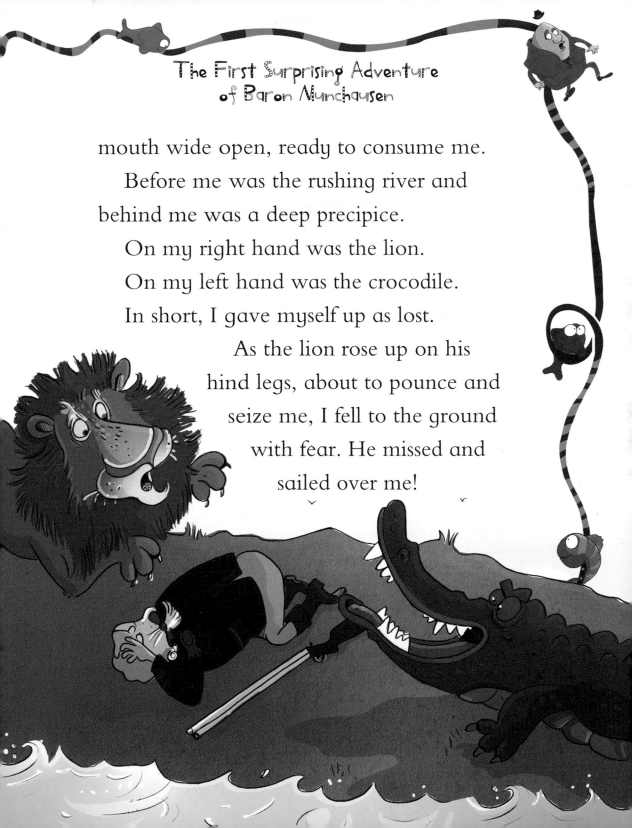

mouth wide open, ready to consume me.

Before me was the rushing river and behind me was a deep precipice.

On my right hand was the lion.

On my left hand was the crocodile.

In short, I gave myself up as lost.

As the lion rose up on his hind legs, about to pounce and seize me, I fell to the ground with fear. He missed and sailed over me!

ABSURD ACCIDENTS

I lay curled up on the ground, shielding my head with my arms, every moment expecting to feel teeth or claws in some part of me. However, after waiting like this for a few seconds, I heard a violent but highly unusual noise, different from any sound that I had ever heard before. Summoning my courage, I ventured to raise my head and look around.

To my unspeakable joy, I saw that the lion had dived straight over me, and into the crocodile's mouth! The lion's head was stuck fast down the crocodile's throat, and the pair were flailing about, struggling to free themselves.

At that very moment, my companion arrived in search of me. He witnessed the

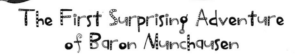

whole strange sight for himself, so if you doubt my word, he can tell you that it is indeed all true.

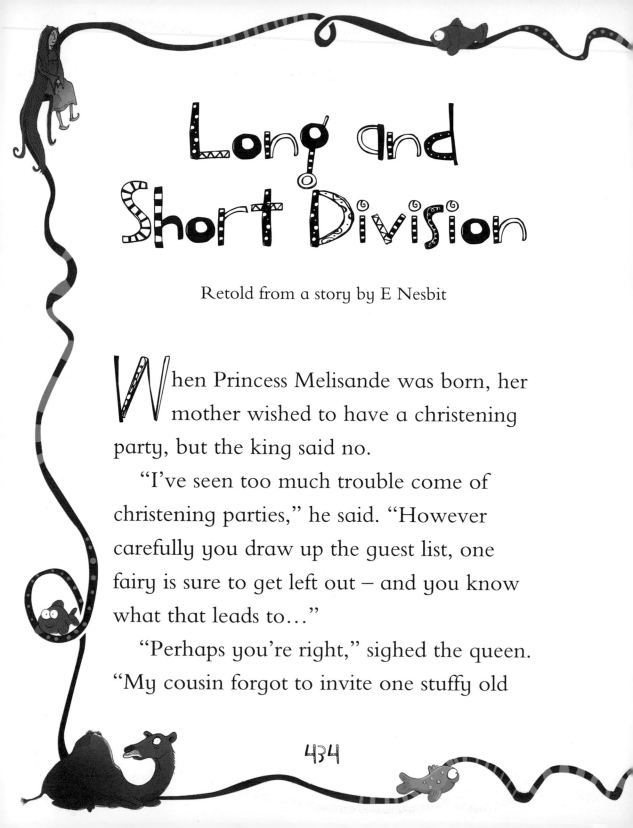

Long and Short Division

Retold from a story by E Nesbit

When Princess Melisande was born, her mother wished to have a christening party, but the king said no.

"I've seen too much trouble come of christening parties," he said. "However carefully you draw up the guest list, one fairy is sure to get left out – and you know what that leads to…"

"Perhaps you're right," sighed the queen. "My cousin forgot to invite one stuffy old fairy to her daughter's christening. The old wretch turned up and the girl drops toads out of her mouth to this day."

"Just so," said the king. "We won't ask a single fairy to the christening – then none of them can be offended."

"Unless they all are," said the queen.

That was just what happened. When the king and queen and baby got back from the christening, the butler met them at the door. "Your Majesties," he said anxiously, "there are seven hundred angry fairies waiting for you in the Throne Room."

With a sigh, the queen opened the door and began: "I'm very sorry—"

"Hold your tongue," interrupted the most wicked fairy, Malevola, very rudely.

"You know what happens if a fairy is left out of a christening party. We are all going to give our presents now. I shall begin… the princess shall be bald."

The queen nearly fainted as Malevola drew back and another fairy in a smart scarlet bonnet with snakes in it stepped forward, ready to curse the baby too. But the king held up his hand firmly.

"Oh no you don't!" he declared. "Have none of you ladies been to fairy school? According to fairy rules, only one bad fairy ever casts a spell at a christening party. So Malevola has spoken and that's it – no one else! Do I make myself clear?"

Several of the older fairies began to murmur that actually the king was right.

"Who's going to risk breaking the rules first?" challenged the king.

No one answered, and the fairies began to slink out of the door.

When the very last fairy had gone, the queen tore off her baby's little lace cap and immediately burst into tears. For all the baby's downy golden hair came away with the cap, and Princess Melisande was as bald as an egg.

"Don't cry, my love," said the king. "I have a wish lying by, which I've never had occasion to use. My fairy godmother gave it to me for a wedding present, but since then I've had nothing to wish for!"

"Thank you, dear," said the queen, smiling through her tears.

"I'll keep the wish until the baby grows up," the king went on. "Then I'll give it to her, and if she would like to wish for hair she can."

So Princess Melisande grew up as beautiful as the sunshine and as good as gold, but never a hair grew on her head. On the day she turned eighteen, the king unlocked his gold safe, took out the wish and gave it to his daughter.

Melisande thought for a moment, then said: "Father, I will wish that all your subjects should be quite happy."

But they were that already, because the king and queen were so good to them. So the wish remained.

So then Melisande said: "I wish them all to be good." But they were that already, because they were happy. So again the wish hung fire.

"Dearest, for my sake, wish what I tell

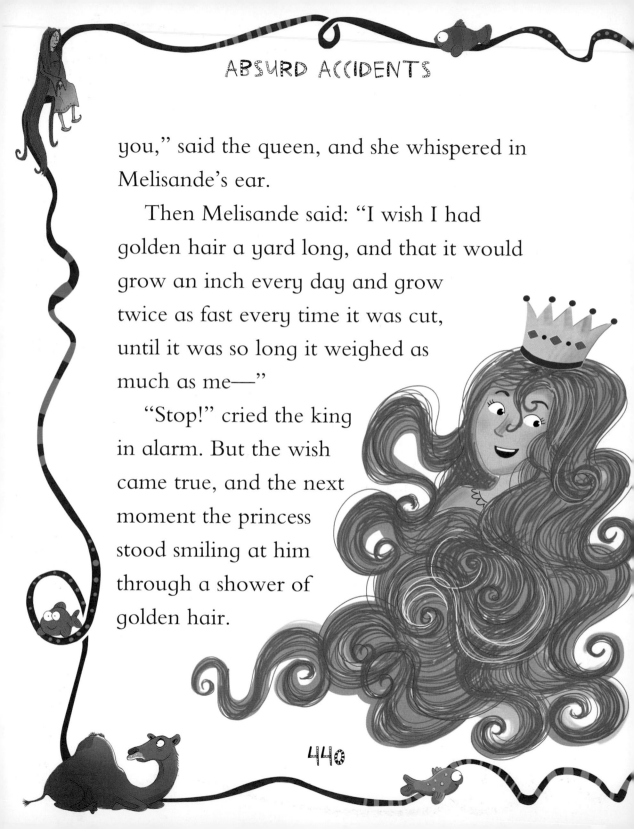

you," said the queen, and she whispered in Melisande's ear.

Then Melisande said: "I wish I had golden hair a yard long, and that it would grow an inch every day and grow twice as fast every time it was cut, until it was so long it weighed as much as me—"

"Stop!" cried the king in alarm. But the wish came true, and the next moment the princess stood smiling at him through a shower of golden hair.

"What's the matter dear?" the queen asked her husband.

"You'll find out soon enough," replied the king.

Indeed they did. The princess's hair began by being a yard long, and it grew an inch every night. In about five weeks her hair was about two yards long. It trailed along the floor and swept up all the dust. And still the princess's hair was growing an inch every night. When it was three yards long it was so heavy and hot that Melisande could not bear it any longer. She took some scissors and cut it all off, and then for a few hours she was comfortable. But the hair went on growing… and now it grew twice as fast as before, so that in thirty-six days it was as long as ever.

The poor princess cried with tiredness. When she couldn't bear it any more she cut her hair and was comfortable for a very short time. For the hair now grew four times as fast. In eighteen days it was as long as before, and she had to have it cut again. Then it grew eight inches a day. And after the next cut it grew sixteen inches a day. And so on, growing twice as fast after each cut, until the princess went to bed at night with her hair clipped short and woke up in the morning with golden hair flowing all about the room. The royal hairdresser had to come and cut the hair off before she could get out of bed.

"Oh I wish I was bald again," sighed

poor Melisande often.

One day, the king came across her weeping. "I shall write to my fairy godmother," he said to the queen, "and see if something cannot be done."

So he sent a letter, and in return came this answer: "Why not advertise for a competent prince? Offer the usual reward."

The king sent out his heralds all over the world to proclaim that any respectable prince could marry Princess Melisande if he could stop her hair growing. From far and near came hordes of princes anxious to give it a go. They brought with them all sorts of nasty remedies, but none of them worked – and Princess Melisande was glad, for she didn't like any of the princes.

One night, Melisande was sitting at her window when she saw a new arrival walking in the garden. For the first time, she found herself wishing that a prince might actually stop her hair from growing.

The prince suddenly looked up. "Are you Melisande?" he asked. "I am Prince Florizel. May I climb up to you?"

"Surely," said the princess. So the prince climbed up a tree to reach her window.

"Now," he said, smiling kindly, "if I can do what your father asks, would you want to marry me?"

"Oh yes," she replied.

"I need a kiss to seal the promise," he said. The princess gladly gave him a kiss… and then another, so as not to be thought mean… and one more – just for luck.

The next day Prince Florizel ordered a pair of giant gold weighing scales to be made. When they were ready, he had them put out in the palace gardens under a big oak tree. Taking Melisande's hand, he helped her up to sit in one side of the scale.

"What will go in the other scale?" asked Melisande.

"Your hair," said Florizel. "You see, your hair has not been able to tell when it's the same weight as you. So, if we measure it, and cut it off at just the right weight, it should not go on growing any more…"

When Melisande was ready, Prince Florizel cut off her hair with his sword, and at once it began to grow at a

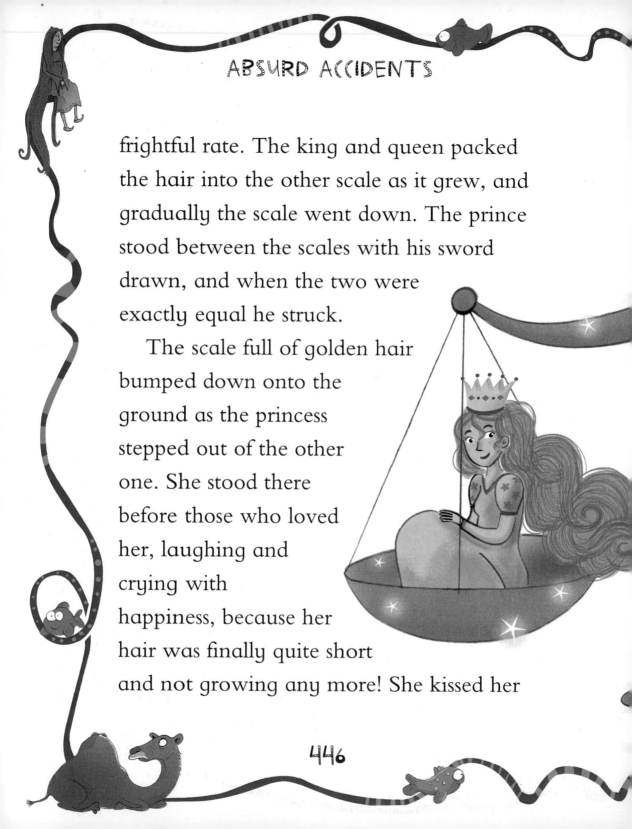

frightful rate. The king and queen packed the hair into the other scale as it grew, and gradually the scale went down. The prince stood between the scales with his sword drawn, and when the two were exactly equal he struck.

The scale full of golden hair bumped down onto the ground as the princess stepped out of the other one. She stood there before those who loved her, laughing and crying with happiness, because her hair was finally quite short and not growing any more! She kissed her prince a hundred and one times, and the next day they were married. And of course, every fairy in the kingdom was invited!

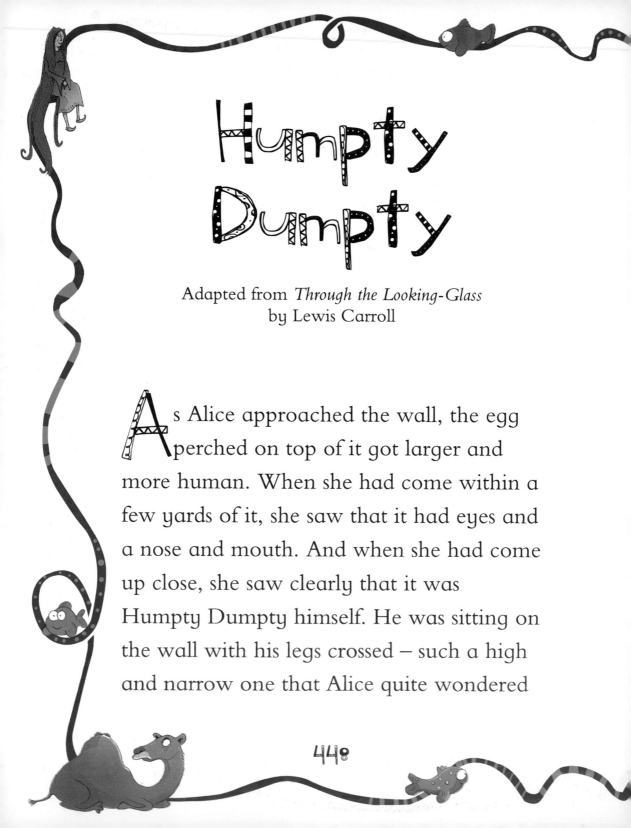

Humpty Dumpty

Adapted from *Through the Looking-Glass*
by Lewis Carroll

As Alice approached the wall, the egg perched on top of it got larger and more human. When she had come within a few yards of it, she saw that it had eyes and a nose and mouth. And when she had come up close, she saw clearly that it was Humpty Dumpty himself. He was sitting on the wall with his legs crossed – such a high and narrow one that Alice quite wondered how he could keep his balance. As he didn't take the least notice of her, she thought he must be a stuffed figure.

"How exactly like an egg he is!" she said, standing with her hands ready to catch him, for she was every moment expecting him to fall.

"It's *very* provoking," Humpty Dumpty said, looking away from Alice as he spoke, "to be called an egg – *very*!"

"I said you *looked* like an egg, sir," Alice gently explained.

"Some people," said Humpty Dumpty, "have no more sense than a baby!"

Alice didn't know what to say to this. It wasn't at all like a conversation, she thought, as he never said anything to her.

In fact, his last remark was evidently addressed to a tree. So she stood and softly repeated to herself:

"'Humpty Dumpty sat on a wall,
Humpty Dumpty had a great fall.
All the King's horses and all the King's men
Couldn't put Humpty Dumpty in his
place again.'

"That last line is much too long for the poetry," she added.

"Don't stand there chattering to yourself like that," Humpty Dumpty said, looking at her for the first time. "Tell me your name and your business."

"My name is Alice, but—"

"It's a stupid enough name!" Humpty Dumpty interrupted impatiently. "What does it mean?"

"*Must* a name mean something?" Alice asked doubtfully.

"Of course it must," Humpty Dumpty said with a short laugh. "*My* name means the shape I am – and a good handsome shape it is, too. With a name like yours, you might be any shape, almost."

"Why do you sit out here all alone?" said Alice, not wishing to begin an argument.

"Why, because there's nobody with me!" cried Humpty Dumpty.

"Don't you think you'd be safer down on the ground?" Alice went on. "That wall is so very narrow!"

"Of course I don't think so!" growled Humpty Dumpty. "Why, if ever I *did* fall off – which there's no chance of – but if I did, the *King* has promised me to—"

"Send all his horses and all his men," Alice interrupted, rather unwisely.

"Now I declare that's too bad!" Humpty Dumpty cried, breaking into a sudden passion. "You've been listening at doors – and behind trees – and down chimneys – or you couldn't have known it!"

"I haven't, indeed!" Alice said very gently. "It's in a book."

"Ah, well! They may write such things in a *book*," Humpty Dumpty said in a calmer tone. "That's what you call a

history of England, that is. *I'm* one that has spoken to a King, I am. However, this conversation is going on a little too fast. Let's go back to the last remark but one."

"I'm afraid I can't quite remember it," Alice said very politely.

"In that case we start fresh," said Humpty Dumpty. "It's your turn to choose a subject…"

"Would you kindly tell me the meaning of the poem called *Jabberwocky*?" said Alice.

"Let's hear it," said Humpty Dumpty. "I can explain all the poems that were ever invented – and a good many that haven't been invented just yet."

This sounded very hopeful, so Alice repeated the first verse:

""'Twas brillig, and the slithy toves
Did gyre and gimble in the wabe,
All mimsy were the borogoves,
And the mome raths outgrabe.'"

"That's enough to begin with," Humpty Dumpty interrupted. "There are plenty of hard words there. 'Brillig' means four o'clock in the afternoon – the time when you begin broiling things for dinner."

"That'll do very well," said Alice. "And what about 'slithy'?"

"Well, 'slithy' means 'lithe and slimy'. 'Lithe' is the same as 'active'. You see, there are two meanings packed up into one word."

"I see it now," Alice remarked

thoughtfully. "And what are 'toves'?"

"Well, 'toves' are something like badgers – they're something like lizards – and they're something like corkscrews."

"They must be very curious creatures."

"They are that," said Humpty Dumpty. "Also they make their nests under sundials – also they live on cheese."

"And what's the 'gyre' and to 'gimble'?"

"To 'gyre' is to go round and round like a gyroscope. To 'gimble' is to make holes like a gimlet."

"And 'the wabe' is the grass-plot round a sundial, I suppose?" said Alice, surprised at her own ingenuity.

"Of course it is. It's called 'wabe', you know, because it goes a long way before it and a long way behind it—"

"And a long way beyond it on each side," Alice added.

"Exactly so. Well, then, 'mimsy' is 'flimsy and miserable'. And a 'borogove' is a thin, shabby-looking bird with its feathers sticking out all round – something like a live mop."

"And then 'mome raths'?" said Alice. "I'm afraid I'm giving you a lot of trouble."

"Well, a 'rath' is a sort of green pig. But 'mome' I'm not certain about. I think it's short for 'from home' – meaning that they'd lost their way, you know."

"And what does 'outgrabe' mean?"

"Well, 'outgrabing' is something between bellowing and whistling, with a kind of sneeze in the middle. However, you'll hear it done, maybe – down in the wood yonder – and when you've once heard it you'll be *quite* content. Who's been repeating all that hard stuff to you?"

"I read it in a book," replied Alice.

"That's all," said Humpty Dumpty. "Goodbye."

'This was rather sudden,' Alice thought, but, after such a strong hint that she ought to be going, she felt that it would hardly be civil to stay. So she held out her hand. "Goodbye, till we meet again!" she said as cheerfully as she could.

Alice waited a minute to see if he would speak again, but as he didn't take further notice of her, she quietly walked away. But she couldn't help saying to herself as she went, "Of all the unsatisfactory people I *ever met*—" She never finished the sentence, for at this moment a heavy crash shook the forest from end to end.

"Oh dear," sighed Alice.

The Sing-Song of Old Man Kangaroo

Adapted from the story by Rudyard Kipling

The Kangaroo was not always as we behold him now. He was once a different animal with four short legs. He was grey and he was woolly, and he was very proud, and he danced on an outcrop in the middle of Australia.

At ten o'clock one day, before

lunchtime, he went to the Big God Nqong, saying, "Make me different from all other animals. Make me, also, popular and truly sought after by five this afternoon."

Up jumped Nqong from his bath in the salt-marsh and shouted, "Yes, I will!"

And Nqong called Dingo – Yellow-Dog Dingo – always hungry, dusty in the sunshine, and showed him Kangaroo. Nqong said, "Dingo! Wake up, Dingo! Do you see that gentleman dancing on an ashpit? He wants to be popular and truly sought after. Dingo, make him SO!"

Up jumped Dingo – Yellow-Dog Dingo – and said, "What, that cat-rabbit?"

Off ran Dingo – Yellow-Dog Dingo – always hungry, running after Kangaroo.

And off went the proud Kangaroo on his four little legs like a bunny.

The proud Kangaroo ran through the desert, he ran through the mountains, he ran through the salt-marshes, he ran through the reed-beds, he ran through the blue gumtrees – he ran till his front legs ached. He had to!

And still ran Dingo – Yellow-Dog Dingo – always hungry, never getting

462

nearer, never getting farther, running after
Kangaroo. He had to!

Still ran Kangaroo – Old Man
Kangaroo. He ran through the long grass,
he ran through the short grass, he ran
through the Tropics of Capricorn and
Cancer – he ran till his hind legs ached.
He had to!

Still ran Dingo – Yellow-Dog Dingo –
hungrier and hungrier, never getting

nearer, never getting farther.

And by and by they came to the Wollgong River.

Now, there wasn't any bridge, and there wasn't any ferry-boat, and Kangaroo didn't know how to get over. So he stood on his legs and hopped.

He had to!

He hopped through the Flinders, he hopped through the Cinders, he hopped through the deserts in the middle of Australia. He hopped like a Kangaroo.

First he hopped one yard, then he hopped three yards, then he hopped five yards, his legs growing stronger, his legs growing longer. He hadn't time for rest or refreshment, and he wanted them greatly.

Still ran Dingo – Yellow-Dog Dingo – very much bewildered, very much hungry, and wondering what in the world or out of it made Old Man Kangaroo hop.

For he hopped like a cricket, like a pea in a saucepan, or a new rubber ball on the floor. He had to!

He tucked up his front legs, he hopped on his hind legs, he stuck out his tail for a balance-weight behind him, and he hopped through the Darling Downs. He had to!

Still ran Dingo – Tired-Dog Dingo – hungrier and hungrier, very much bewildered, and wondering when in the world or out of it would Old Man Kangaroo stop.

Then at last came Nqong from his bath

in the salt-marsh, and announced, "It's
five o'clock."

Down sat Dingo – Poor-Dog Dingo –
always hungry, dusky in the sunshine, and
he hung out his tongue and howled.

Down sat Kangaroo – Old Man
Kangaroo – stuck out his tail like a
milking-stool behind him, and said,
"Thank goodness that's finished!"

Then Nqong, who is always a
gentleman, said, "Why aren't
you grateful to Yellow-Dog
Dingo? Why don't you

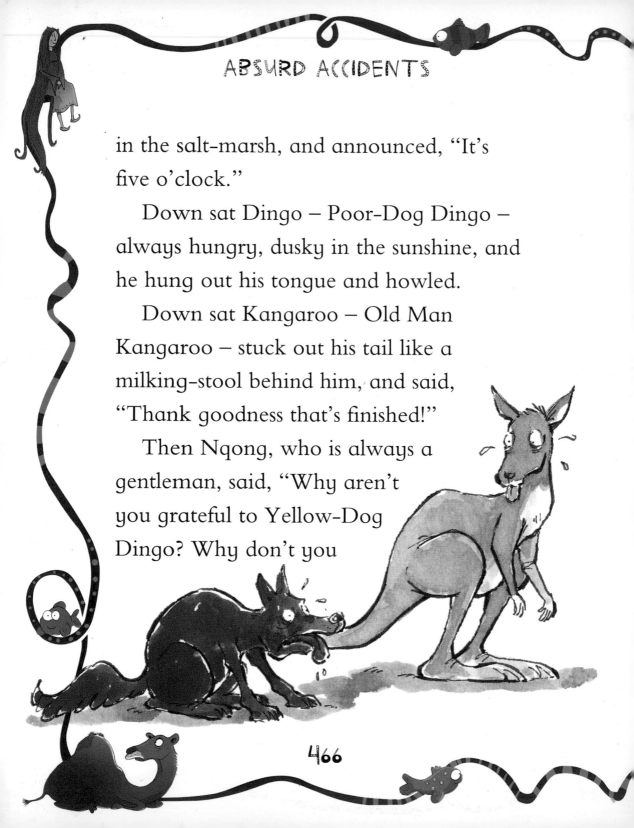

thank him for all he has done for you?"

Then said Kangaroo – Tired Old Kangaroo – "He's chased me out of the homes of my childhood, he's chased me out of my regular mealtimes, he's altered my shape so I'll never get it back, and he's made my legs ache."

Then said Nqong, "Perhaps I'm mistaken, but didn't you ask me to make you different from all other animals, as well as to make you very truly sought after? And now it is five o'clock."

"Yes," said Kangaroo. "I wish that I hadn't. I thought you would do it by charms and incantations, but this is a practical joke."

"Joke!" said Nqong from his bath in

the salt-marsh. "Say that again and I'll whistle up Dingo and run your hind legs off for sure."

"No!" said the Kangaroo. "I must apologize. Legs are legs, and you needn't alter them as far as I am concerned. I only meant to explain to Your Lordliness that I've had nothing to eat since morning, and I'm very empty indeed."

"Yes," said Dingo – Yellow-Dog Dingo – "I am in just the same situation. I've made him different from all other animals, but what may I have for my tea?"

Then said Nqong from his bath in the salt-marsh, "Come and ask me about it tomorrow – I'm going to wash."

So there they were left in the middle of

the desert in Australia, Old Man Kangaroo
and Yellow-Dog Dingo, and each said,
"That's your fault."

A Fish Story

An Australian traditional tale told
by Andrew Lang

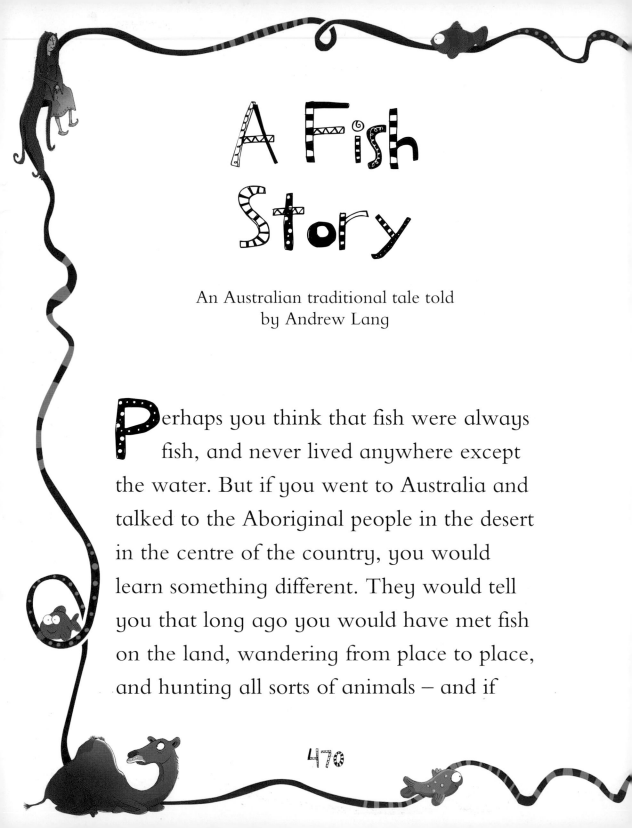

Perhaps you think that fish were always fish, and never lived anywhere except the water. But if you went to Australia and talked to the Aboriginal people in the desert in the centre of the country, you would learn something different. They would tell you that long ago you would have met fish on the land, wandering from place to place, and hunting all sorts of animals – and if you consider how fish are made, you will understand how difficult this must have been and how clever they were to do it. Indeed, so clever were they that they might have been hunting still if a terrible thing had not happened.

One day the whole fish tribe came back very tired from a hunting expedition, and looked about for a nice, cool spot to pitch their camp. It was very hot, so they settled under the branches of a large tree, which grew by a river. They made their fire on the steep riverbank, and while the food was cooking they all stretched themselves out lazily under the tree.

They were just dropping off to sleep when a big black cloud spread over the sun

and rain began to fall. The fire was put out
– and to make matters worse, an icy wind
began to blow and the poor fish were
chilled right through their bodies.

"This will never do," said Thuggai, the
oldest of the fish tribe. "We shall die of cold
unless we can light the fire again." His sons
rubbed two sticks
together till

they were exhausted, but not a single spark could they make.

"Let me try," cried Bernuga, the bony fish, but he had no better luck, and no more had Kumbal, the bream, nor any of the rest.

"It is no use," said Thuggai at last. "The wood is too wet. We must just sit and wait till the sun comes out again and dries it."

Then a very little fish indeed, the youngest of the tribe, came and bowed before Thuggai. "Ask my father, Guddhu the cod, to light the fire," he suggested. "He is skilled in magic more than most fish."

So Thuggai asked Guddhu, and Guddhu stripped some pieces of bark off a tree, and placed them on top of the smouldering ashes. Then he knelt by the side of the fire and blew at it for a long while, till slowly the feeble red glow became a little stronger and the edges of the bark started to curl up.

When the rest of the tribe saw this they pressed close, keeping their backs towards the piercing wind, but Guddhu told them they must go to the other side, as he wanted the wind to fan the fire.

By and by the glow became a flame, and soon sparks were darting from the merrily crackling fire.

"More wood!" cried Guddhu, and they all ran and gathered wood and heaped it onto the flames, which leapt and roared.

"We shall soon be warm now," said the fish, one to another. "Guddhu is truly

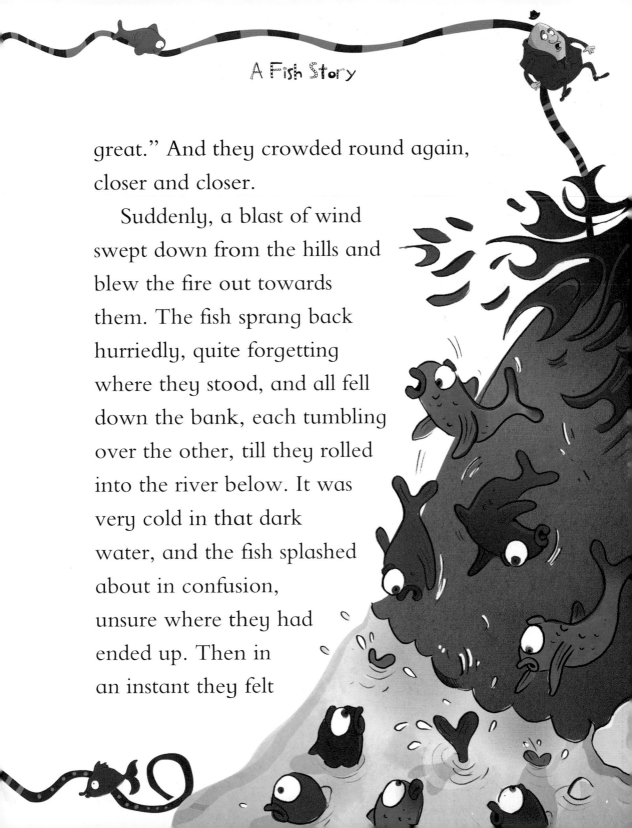

great." And they crowded round again, closer and closer.

Suddenly, a blast of wind swept down from the hills and blew the fire out towards them. The fish sprang back hurriedly, quite forgetting where they stood, and all fell down the bank, each tumbling over the other, till they rolled into the river below. It was very cold in that dark water, and the fish splashed about in confusion, unsure where they had ended up. Then in an instant they felt warm again, for the fire, driven by the strong wind, had followed them right down to the bottom of the river, where it burned as brightly as ever. And the fish gathered round it as they had done on the riverbank. They found the flames just as hot as before, and the fire never went out, like those upon land, but kept on burning forever.

So now you know why, if you dive deep down below the cold surface of the water on a frosty day, you will find it comfortable and pleasant underneath, and be quite sorry that you cannot stay there with the fish.

Jugemu Jugemu

A Japanese folk tale

Long ago, a couple in Japan had a beautiful baby boy. However, they could not agree on a suitable name. So the father went to the temple and asked the chief priest if he could name their son.

The priest suggested several names: Jugemu – meaning 'limitless life', similarly Go-ko-no-surikire – meaning 'unending years', Kaijari-suigyo – meaning 'countless luck and fortune', and Suigy-matsu and

Unraimatsu and Furaimatsu – all meaning 'boundless wellbeing'. He also suggested Kuunerutokoro and Sumutokoro – meaning 'blessed with places to eat and sleep' and Yaburakoji-no-burakoji – meaning 'unending energy'. Alternatively, there were the names Paipo, Shuringan,

Gurindai, Ponpokopi, Ponpokona – all royal names, Chokyumei – meaning 'long and lasting life', and Chosuke – meaning 'blessed for a long time'.

The father thought that the names were all wonderful, and so did the mother – once again, they could not choose between them. So the couple decided to use all the names. Because the priest had said 'Jugemu' first, they thought they should use that name twice. So they called their son: Jugemu Jugemu Go-ko-no-surikire Kaijari-suigyo Suigy-matsu Unraimatsu Furaimatsu Kuunerutokoro Sumutokoro Yaburakoji-no-burakoji Paipo Shuringan Gurindai Ponpokopi Ponpokona Chokyumei Chosuke.

ABSURD ACCIDENTS

Now one day, Jugemu Jugemu Go-ko-no-surikire Kaijari-suigyo Suigy-matsu Unraimatsu Furaimatsu Kuunerutokoro Sumutokoro Yaburakoji-no-burakoji Paipo Shuringan Gurindai Ponpokopi Ponpokona Chokyumei Chosuke was playing with his friend at the edge of a lake when he tripped over a tree root, fell into the water, and began to drown.

"Help! Help!" cried his horrified friend, and he ran round the corner to Jugemu Jugemu Go-ko-no-surikire Kaijari-suigyo Suigy-matsu Unraimatsu Furaimatsu Kuunerutokoro Sumutokoro Yaburakoji-no-burakoji Paipo Shuringan Gurindai Ponpokopi Ponpokona Chokyumei Chosuke's house.

"Jugemu Jugemu Go-ko-no-surikire Kaijari-suigyo Suigy-matsu Unraimatsu Furaimatsu Kuunerutokoro Sumutokoro Yaburakoji-no-burakoji Paipo Shuringan Gurindai Ponpokopi Ponpokona Chokyumei Chosuke has fallen into the lake and he's drowning!" he shouted.

Jugemu Jugemu Go-ko-no-surikire Kaijari-suigyo Suigy-matsu Unraimatsu Furaimatsu Kuunerutokoro Sumutokoro Yaburakoji-no-burakoji Paipo Shuringan Gurindai Ponpokopi Ponpokona Chokyumei Chosuke's mother heard the child's anguished cries and yelled to her husband: "Help! Help! Jugemu Jugemu Go-ko-no-surikire Kaijari-suigyo Suigy-matsu Unraimatsu Furaimatsu Kuunerutokoro

Sumutokoro Yaburakoji-no-burakoji Paipo Shuringan Gurindai Ponpokopi Ponpokona Chokyumei Chosuke has fallen into the lake and is drowning!"

The father jumped to his feet and bellowed to his neighbour: "Quick! Quick! Fetch your ladder! Jugemu Jugemu Go-ko-no-surikire Kaijari-suigyo Suigy-matsu Unraimatsu Furaimatsu Kuunerutokoro Sumutokoro Yaburakoji-no-burakoji Paipo Shuringan Gurindai Ponpokopi Ponpokona Chokyumei Chosuke has fallen into the lake and is drowning!"

And the neighbour shouted to his neighbour, who had borrowed his ladder only yesterday: "Hurry! Hurry! Bring my ladder back! Jugemu Jugemu Go-ko-no-

surikire Kaijari-suigyo Suigy-matsu
Unraimatsu Furaimatsu Kuunerutokoro
Sumutokoro Yaburakoji-no-
burakoji Paipo Shuringan
Gurindai Ponpokopi
Ponpokona Chokyumei
Chosuke has fallen
into the lake
and is drowning!"

The horrified
neighbour brought the
ladder at once, and
everyone ran to
the lake as fast
as their legs would carry
them – and they managed to get Jugemu
Jugemu Go-ko-no-surikire Kaijari-suigyo

Suigy-matsu Unraimatsu Furaimatsu
Kuunerutokoro Sumutokoro Yaburakoji-
no-burakoji Paipo Shuringan Gurindai
Ponpokopi Ponpokona Chokyumei
Chosuke out of the water. It had taken
them all so long to say his name that he
had very nearly drowned.

And that is why, from then on, the
Japanese have always stuck to shorter,
more sensible names.

The Nose

Adapted from the story
by Penrhyn W Coussens

Three soldiers were journeying home from war when one night they found themselves having to pitch their camp in a deep, gloomy wood. To be safe, they agreed to take it in turns to stay awake and keep watch. So two lay down and fell fast asleep, and the other made himself a fire.

He had not been sitting there long, when

suddenly a little man in a red jacket approached. The soldier willingly let the little man sit down and warm himself. The man was so grateful that he took out an old cloak and gave it to the soldier. "When you put this on, anything you wish for will come true," he whispered. He bowed and walked away.

Soon, it was the second soldier's turn to keep watch. It wasn't long before the little man in the red jacket arrived again. This soldier also treated him kindly and in return, he gave the soldier a purse that would always remain full of gold.

Then came the third soldier's turn to take watch.

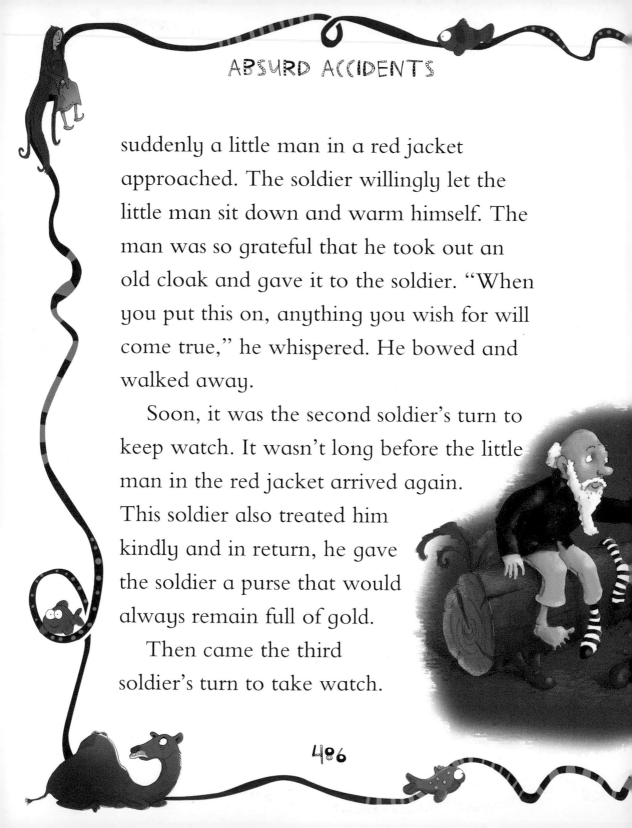

He also welcomed the little man, and was given a wonderful horn that, when blown, could allow the player to control the minds and deeds of others.

The soldiers used their wonderful gifts to travel and see the world, until one day they began to tire of the roving life and thought they should like a home of their own. So the first soldier put his cloak on and wished for a fine castle – in a moment it stood before them.

The soldiers enjoyed their new home for a time, until again they grew restless for adventure. So they took their rich clothes and

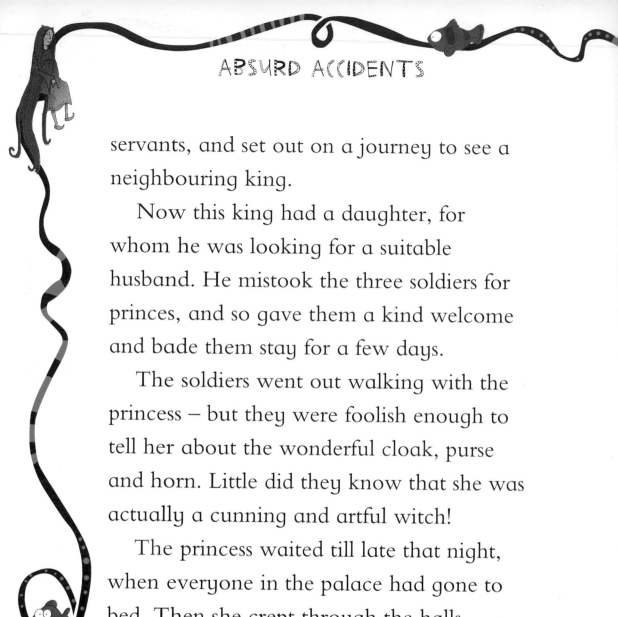

servants, and set out on a journey to see a neighbouring king.

Now this king had a daughter, for whom he was looking for a suitable husband. He mistook the three soldiers for princes, and so gave them a kind welcome and bade them stay for a few days.

The soldiers went out walking with the princess – but they were foolish enough to tell her about the wonderful cloak, purse and horn. Little did they know that she was actually a cunning and artful witch!

The princess waited till late that night, when everyone in the palace had gone to bed. Then she crept through the halls singing a song of enchantment that put everyone into a deep sleep. She crept into

the soldiers' rooms and swapped the
magical cloak, purse and horn for a cloak,
purse and horn that looked just like them!

The three poor fellows did not discover
that anything was amiss until they had
returned to their own castle, opened their
purse for more money, and found it empty.
Then they found that the cloak and the
horn also did nothing. Had the gifts just lost
their magic? Or had the princess betrayed
them? They knew the truth in their hearts.

They were deep in despair when they
heard a sudden knock at the castle door. It
was the little man in the red jacket!

"Why, how now, friends?" he said,
chuckling. "I must help you once again, I
see." He told them to gather some apples

and pears from the fruit trees in the castle grounds. "If someone eats one of the apples their nose will grow… and grow… and grow. But if you give them a pear, it will go back to normal," the little man explained. "Go to the princess and get her to eat some of your apples – her nose will grow twenty times as long and you will be able to get the magic objects back."

They thanked their old friend heartily for his kindness and wisdom. The first soldier dressed himself as a gardener and went to the king's palace, and said he had some remarkable apples to sell. Everyone that saw the shiny red fruit wanted a taste, but he said the apples were for the princess only – she soon sent her maid to buy his

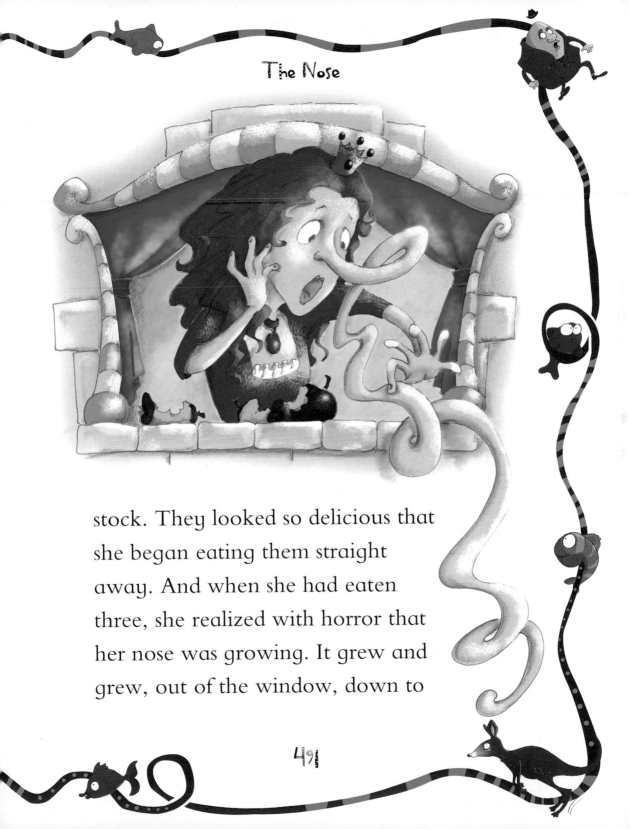

The Nose

stock. They looked so delicious that she began eating them straight away. And when she had eaten three, she realized with horror that her nose was growing. It grew and grew, out of the window, down to the ground, and across the garden to nobody knows where.

The king issued a proclamation that whoever could heal this dreadful disease should be richly rewarded. Many tried, but the princess got no relief.

The second soldier then disguised himself as a doctor and said he could cure her. He chopped up another apple and gave her a dose, to punish her wickedness a little more. He promised to call again tomorrow.

The next day came, and as of course the nose had been growing fast all night, the princess was in a dreadful panic. The soldier chopped up just a tiny amount of the pear for her, and declared he was sure that would help, and that he would call again the next day.

The next day came, and although the nose was a little smaller, it was still bigger than when the 'doctor' first attended to her.

'I must frighten this cunning princess a little more still,' he thought. So he gave her a little more of the chopped apple and said he would call again the next day.

The next day the nose was much bigger than before, and the 'doctor' told the princess and king: "Something is working against my medicine – I believe it is too strong for it."

He called a priest – really the third soldier in disguise – and the priest said: "I know what the matter is. You possess stolen goods! If you do not return them, there is no hope for you – you will die."

Then the wicked princess was very frightened and ordered her maid to fetch the cloak, purse and horn at once. She gave them to the 'priest', and begged him to return them to the soldiers. As soon as he had the magic objects back safe he gave her a whole pear to eat, and the nose returned to its proper shape.

The 'doctor' and the 'priest' were soon back with their friend, the 'gardener'. And they all lived happily ever after in their castle, from which princesses, apples and pears were completely forbidden.

The Magician's Heart

Adapted from the story by E Nesbit

We all have our weaknesses. Mine is
jewellery. Yours, perhaps, sweets.
Professor Taykin's was royal events.
Believing himself much more important
than he was, he always expected to be
asked to the birthday parties, weddings and
christenings of all the royals, near and far.
Of course he never was, because he was not

a lord or a duke, but a wicked magician.

Well, at last he went to a christening anyway, without being asked. It was a very grand party given by the king of the Fortunate Islands, and the little prince was christened Fortunatus. And when all the bright, laughing fairy godmothers were crowding round the blue satin cradle, giving gifts of beauty and strength and kindness to the baby, the magician performed a very difficult charm (in his head, like you do mental arithmetic), and then declared: "I say young Forty shall be the stupidest prince in the world." With that he vanished in a puff of red smoke.

Taykin very much enjoyed knowing that he had made such a lot of people unhappy, and the next Wednesday he went uninvited to another royal christening. This time the baby was a girl. Taykin kept close to the pink velvet cradle and, when all the good qualities in the world had been given to the princess, he did another charm and then announced: "I say Little Aura shall be the ugliest princess in all the world."

And instantly she was. It was terrible.

The magician did the spell (in his mind, just as you do your spelling) to make himself vanish, but to his horror there was no smoke and he remained where he was – one of the fairies had cast a

497

strong charm to prevent his vanishing. (This fairy was a white witch, and of course you know that white magic is stronger than black magic.)

The dear white witch bent down and kissed the baby princess. "There!" she said. "You can keep that kiss till you need it."

The wicked magician was shut up in an enormously high tower surrounded by an enchantment from the white witch, so he could play with magic inside the tower but could not use it to get out.

And so the years passed. Professor Taykin stayed in the tower and did magic and was very bored. Prince Fortunatus was such a stupid young man that he went about thinking his name was James, and telling people so. Aura remained hideous. She was very unhappy – until on her twentieth birthday she struck upon an idea.

Now that very morning Professor Taykin's old nurse decided to pay him a visit. In her old age she had been thinking about how delightful Taykin had been as a baby, and had started to feel sorry for him. Taykin was pleased to see her – after all, she was the only visitor he had had in twenty years.

"Aren't you lonely?" asked the nurse.

"Yes," admitted the magician. He sniffed, conjured himself a handkerchief out of empty air, and wiped his eyes.

"Well, I've brought you an apprentice, my dear," said the nurse, and she went out and brought in James, who was really the Prince of the Fortunate Islands.

The magician was delighted, realizing at once who the young man was. Before he could celebrate, there was a knock at the door. "Go on then, stupid," the magician ordered James, who went and opened it.

A girl stood there wearing a tattered servant's dress, her face covered by a veil.

"Please," said the girl, who was of course Princess Aura, "is Professor Taykin here?"

"Snakes alive!" said Taykin. "Three visitors – what a day I'm having!"

"You see, it's like this," said the veiled princess. "I'm so ugly no one can bear to look at me. I can't go out in public unless I disguise myself, as it's so shameful to be an ugly princess. I thought perhaps you could make me pretty. I happen to have fifty pounds – I'll give it to you for a new face."

"Done," cried the greedy Taykin. He grabbed the money, waved his wand, and the ugly princess became the loveliest girl in the world.

"Wow!" said the nurse.

"Wow!" repeated the apprentice.

"How can I thank you?" cried the overjoyed princess.

"Quite easily," said the magician, "you can marry me. I hereby offer you my hand and heart."

He put his hand into his waistcoat and pulled out his heart. It was fat and pink, and the princess did not much like the look of it.

"Thank you very much," she said, wrinkling her pretty nose, "but actually my affections have recently been engaged," and she glanced shyly at James. "I can't marry you."

"Very well," spat the magician, "then I will cast my worst magic upon you. Nurse, come and help me carry in my potions."

He went into the next room, the nurse with him.

"He shan't cast his worst magic upon you – I will fight him!" vowed James. "I may be stupid but I'm strong too."

"How brave you are," said Aura admiringly. She kissed him – and all of a sudden his stupidness passed away like a cloud. He knew who he was, and he knew he was as clever as anyone. He also knew that he had fallen in love with the princess.

"That was a magic kiss, you know," she told him. "My fairy godmother gave it to me." And she slipped quickly out of the front door just as Taykin came back through the other.

He was furious to find her gone. I should

not like to write down the things he yelled at his apprentice! But then in a strange, confused, yet quite definite way, he felt the white witch's enchantment around the tower disappear. His extreme fury had caused it to dissolve.

"To the palace!" he cried. And, bellowing some magic words, he leapt to the window and vanished.

Without a moment's hesitation, Prince Fortunatus (for that was who he really was) followed him. He felt himself vanish – a most uncomfortable sensation – and reappear, at the back door of the palace.

It had taken no time at all, yet the magician had already succeeded in obtaining a job as palace cook.

Taykin's annoyance at being followed quickly disappeared as he realized he could set his stupid and faithful (or so he thought) apprentice to work as his scullion. He ordered Fortunatus to scrub surfaces and wash up, while he leapt about the kitchen, conjuring a magnificent dinner of seventeen courses from totally empty saucepans.

"Phew! All this excitement today is bad for my heart, I think," Taykin said. He pulled his heart out of his chest and put it on a nearby shelf. As he did so, an unfortunate accident occurred (unfortunate for the magician, anyway) – his notebook containing his most inventive spells fell from his pocket, and Fortunatus picked it up. Taykin did not see him do it – he was too busy making a ladle fly about the room.

It was just then that Aura came in, looking more lovely than ever. "I've come to give the orders for dinner," she said. But when she saw who it was, she gave a little cry and stood rooted to the spot, trembling.

"Aha! It's you!" cried the magician, his eyes gleaming. "You must marry me! And if you say no, I'll return you to ugliness as soon as the word leaves your lips."

"I'll tell Papa," said the sobbing princess.

"No, you won't," said Taykin. "Your father will never know." He caught her by the wrist.

"Stop!" cried Fortunatus. "I've got your heart!" He had – he held it up in one hand, a kitchen knife in the other. "One more step," he warned, "and in goes the knife."

"When did you stop being stupid?" the astonished magician spat. Then he remembered his unfortunate predicament. "I say, look out!" he cried. "That's my heart you've got there. My life's bound up in it, so be careful!"

"I know. That's often the case with people's hearts," said Fortunatus. "We've got you, my dear professor, on toast. Utter just one word and before you can finish the spell it will be curtains for you. My princess, might I trouble you to call the guards?"

And so the guards arrested the magician and Fortunatus gave them his heart, so he dare not try to escape. A new palace cook was appointed and a very good dinner was

served, over which the king told the
princess how delighted he was that she had
found such a brave, clever prince to marry.
Then at last the guards hauled the
magician before the king. He wondered
what to do with him.

"I could take the badness out of him,"
suggested Fortunatus. "There's an excellent
spell in this notebook – but if I did that
there wouldn't be very much of him left."

"Can't be helped," shrugged the king.

So Fortunatus studied the book for a few
moments and then said some words in a
strange language.

As he spoke, the wicked magician began
to tremble and shrink, growing smaller and
smaller until in his place stood a chubby,

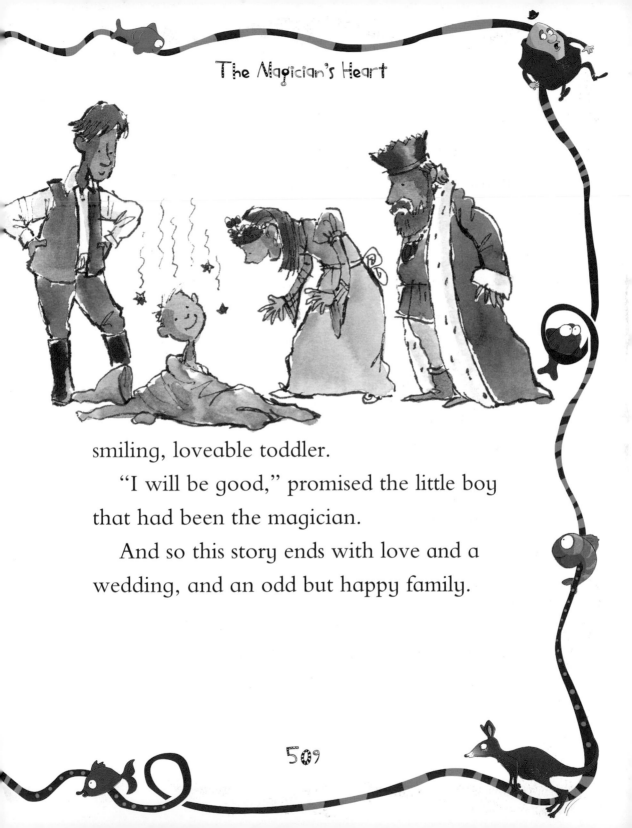

smiling, loveable toddler.

"I will be good," promised the little boy
that had been the magician.

And so this story ends with love and a
wedding, and an odd but happy family.

About the Authors

AESOP *c.* 620–560 BC

Many people think Aesop was a slave in ancient Greece – and such a brilliant storyteller that he was eventually rewarded with his freedom. He has been credited with creating more than 600 fables – short stories that teach a lesson.

HANS CHRISTIAN ANDERSEN 1805–1875

Born in Denmark, Hans Christian Andersen has become famous worldwide for his children's tales, many of which have been translated into over 150 languages.

LEWIS CARROLL 1832–1898

'Lewis Carroll' was the pen name of Charles Lutwidge Dodgson. He was a mathematician at Oxford University. He is most famous for his 'Alice' novels, but also wrote poetry and short stories.

KENNETH GRAHAME 1859–1932

Born in Scotland, Grahame grew up in Berkshire, England, near the river Thames. He is best known for his children's novel, *The Wind in the Willows*, which has become a classic.

JACOB LUDWIG KARL GRIMM 1785–1863
WILHELM KARL GRIMM 1786–1859

Born near Frankfurt in Germany, the Grimm brothers read law at university, then studied spoken language and how it changes over time. They collected and published over 200 European folk tales.

JOEL CHANDLER HARRIS 1848–1908

Harris lived in Georgia, North America. As a teenager, he left school to work as a printer's apprentice. He later wrote fiction and retold folklore, including many 'Brer Rabbit' stories from the African-American oral tradition.

JOSEPH JACOBS 1854–1916

Jacobs was born in Australia and studied in England and Germany, researching Jewish history. He settled in America and, inspired by the Grimm brothers, went on to edit five collections of fairytales.

RUDYARD KIPLING 1865–1936

Born to a British family in India, Kipling lived in England from the age of five, where he was educated. He became one of Britain's best-loved poets and writers for works including *Just So Stories* and *The Jungle Book*.

ANDREW LANG 1844–1912

Born in Scotland, Lang studied at St Andrew's University in Fife and Balliol College, Oxford. He researched folklore, mythology and religion, and wrote poetry, novels and literary criticism. Lang adapted many folk and fairytales for children in a series of 12 books.

E NESBIT 1858–1924

Famous for novels such as *The Railway Children* and *Five Children and It*, Nesbit was born in Surrey, England. She wrote and collaborated on over 60 children's books.

MARK TWAIN 1835–1910

'Mark Twain' was the pen name of Samuel Langhorne Clemens, who grew up in Missouri, North America. Twain became a journalist and also wrote funny sketches and stories. He is most famous for the novels *The Adventures of Tom Sawyer* and *Adventures of Huckleberry Finn*.

OSCAR WILDE 1854–1900

Wilde was born in Dublin, Ireland. He studied at Oxford University then moved to London, where he moved in fashionable social circles. He wrote poetry, short stories and plays – many of which have become classics, such as *The Importance of Being Earnest*.

511

About the Artists

Kathryn Durst grew up in Peterborough, Canada, and has been drawing ever since she could hold a pencil. She works in a variety of styles, using both traditional and digital mediums. Her art has been described as charming and expressive. Kathryn works on children's books and television series, and is also a puppeteer, animator and film-maker.

Michael Garton lives with his wife, daughter and dalmatian on the Wirral in northwest England. He gained a degree in illustration for children's publishing in 2004, and has been illustrating children's books ever since. He thinks everyone should live their own brilliant funny stories.

Mike Phillips was born in London long ago, when TVs didn't have colour and phones were so big you had to carry them in a wheelbarrow. He learned to draw by copying characters from his favourite comics, and now lives in Devon with his wife, three children, a dog and three cats.

Mirella Mariani has been in love with drawing since she can remember. She was born in a small green village between Milan and Como, Italy. As a child, she loved books and comics, and now illustrates them – she is most interested in their humour. Mirella enjoys cycling, horse riding and scuba diving and also loves animals, including drawing them!

Stevee Stone was born in the northeast of England, and now lives and works in Derbyshire with his wife and Vincent, a very cheeky ginger cat. He illustrates all sorts of things, although animals are his favourite subject – they inspire most of his picture books and paintings.

Tina Perko was born in Ljubljana, Slovenia, in 1971. She has a degree in fashion design from the Istituto Marangoni in Milan, Italy. For the last 10 years she has been illustrating children's picture books and writing stories, and has also contributed to children's magazines. Today, Tina is a well-established illustrator.